Friends, Foes and Felonies

Sapphire Beach Cozy Mystery Series
(Book 9)

Angela K. Ryan

John Paul Publishing

TEWKSBURY, MASSACHUSETTS

Angela K. Ryan
John Paul Publishing
Post Office Box 283
Tewksbury, MA 01876

Publisher's Note: This is a work of fiction. Names, characters, places, and incidents are a product of the author's imagination. Locales and public names are sometimes used for atmospheric purposes. Any resemblance to actual people, living or dead, or to businesses, companies, events, institutions, or locales is completely coincidental.

Cover Design © 2020 MariahSinclair.com
Book Layout © 2017 BookDesignTemplates.com

Friends, Foes and Felonies/ Angela K. Ryan. -- 1st ed.
ISBN: 978-1-7353064-5-2

A Note of Thanks from the Author

I would like to warmly thank all those who generously shared their time and knowledge in the research of this book, especially:

Jacki Strategos, Premier Sotheby's
International Realty, Marco Island

Carol Buccieri
Bella Stella Beads, Haverhill, Massachusetts

Marco Island Fire Rescue
Marco Island, Florida

Any errors are my own.

Chapter 1

CONNIE CLUTCHED Zach's hand and practically pulled him through the parking garage, across the street, and into Concourse D at Southwest Florida International Airport.

They climbed the staircase and made their way toward a wooden bench. Connie anxiously glanced at the corridor that Sam O'Neil, her longtime friend and mentor, would be required to pass through upon arriving. On one side was a large window and on the other was the security checkpoint for departing passengers.

"Let's wait here," Connie said, plopping herself down on the empty bench.

Zach pulled his phone from his pocket and glanced at the time. "We're early. It will be at least ten more minutes before Sam arrives. His plane is probably just touching ground now."

Connie let out a sharp breath. "I know. I just wanted to be sure we were here to greet him the second he arrived. I can't believe it's been nearly two years since I last saw him. For eleven years, Sam and I worked side-by-side in the office. And that doesn't even include the countless weekend fundraisers and business trips."

Connie's eleven years working for Sam at *Feeding the Hungry*, a non-profit agency that served the poor in various developing countries, as well as her post-graduate term of volunteer service in Kenya, gave her the confidence and experience to open *Just Jewelry*, the shop where she sold Fair Trade jewelry and her own handmade pieces.

Zach rested his arm on Connie's shoulders. "I'm looking forward to meeting someone who has been such an important part of your life."

Connie leaned against Zach. "It was actually my parents who introduced us. Did I ever tell you the story?"

"I don't think so."

"Sam was one of my father's clients. My dad was his personal accountant. When Sam would go to my dad's office every year to get his taxes done, my father would keep him posted on my adventures in Kenya. Shortly after I returned, Sam called my dad to tell him that he decided to close his lucrative consulting business to start a non-profit organization after participating in a humanitarian trip to South America with his parish. He wanted to hire my father to take care of the organization's accounting needs. My dad thought Sam and I would enjoy meeting each other, so my parents invited Sam and his wife, Janet, to Sunday dinner one afternoon. By the end of the meal, Sam had offered me a job and I had accepted."

"And the rest is history?"

"Exactly. I'm looking forward to spending the next two weeks with him. Sam is a combination of an older brother and a second father to me. I have a feeling something meaningful will happen while he's in Sapphire Beach."

"What do you mean by that?" Zach asked.

Connie shrugged her shoulders. "It's hard to explain, exactly, but it's always a blessing when Sam and I get together. We're like kindred spirits, even though he is twenty years older than me. There's usually some sort of strange parallel with what's going on in each of our lives, ever since he opened *Feeding the Hungry.* At that time, I was trying to figure out a path for my life that would somehow be a continuation of my work in Africa, and Sam was wondering how'd he grow a non-profit with no help."

Zach kissed the top of Connie's head. "It sounds like you two have a special bond."

"I couldn't believe it when he told me he was coming for two weeks. As long as I've known Sam, he's never taken that much time off from work. I also can't wait to run by him the plans I've made for the expansion of my Fair Trade section. I'm sure he'll have some great ideas."

Connie couldn't sit still, so she walked to the airport monitors and checked on the latest flight information, then eagerly returned to Zach. "His flight landed ten minutes ago. It shouldn't be long now."

A minute later, Connie jumped up and pointed toward the corridor. "There he is!"

Before Zach could say a word, Connie darted toward a man with salt and pepper hair, a medium build, and kind blue eyes. She threw her arms around his neck. Until that moment, Connie hadn't realized just how much she had missed her old friend and mentor.

Zach caught up with Connie and Sam.

"Let me guess," Zach said. "This is Sam."

A smile was plastered on Connie's face. "Nah, I just like to give perfect strangers a warm welcome to Florida," she joked.

Zach extended his hand. "Hi Sam, I'm Zach. I feel like I know you already from everything Connie has told me about you."

Sam pushed away Zach's hand and pulled him into a warm hug. "And I, you. It's a pleasure to finally meet the man who captured Connie's heart."

Zach glanced at Connie and smiled broadly. Then he took the backpack Sam had been carrying.

"Thank you, Zach," Sam said.

"It's the least I can do for a weary traveler. I'll bet you're exhausted."

Connie had been so excited to see Sam that she hadn't noticed how tired he looked until Zach mentioned it. Dark circles had formed beneath his eyes, and his skin tone was paler than normal, even for a long New England winter. Sam had only taken a quick three-and-a-half-hour direct flight from Boston, so he shouldn't have been nearly as tired as he appeared.

Connie placed her hand on Sam's forearm. "Come to think of it, you do look weary. Let's pick up your luggage and get you settled in at home so you can rest. Dinner is ready to be put in the oven."

After retrieving Sam's suitcase at Carousel 10, they walked back to the parking garage and loaded Sam's suitcase into Zach's grey Jeep. Within forty minutes, they had pulled into the underground garage at Palm Paradise, which was the condo building where Connie lived. They ascended the elevator to the seventh floor and entered Connie's condo.

Connie's chestnut and white Cavalier King Charles Spaniel eagerly trotted over to greet them.

"This must be Ginger," Sam said, bending over to return the dog's affection. He reached into the front pocket of his suitcase and pulled out a rawhide bone with a red ribbon tied around it. He took off the ribbon and gave the bone to the dog.

"A belated Christmas gift," Sam said.

Zach smiled. "I think you just made a friend for life. That is so thoughtful of you."

Connie and Sam both chuckled at Zach's comment.

"What's so funny?"

"Sam is a generous guy, but the gift for Ginger was undoubtedly courtesy of his wife, Janet," Connie clarified.

"Don't get me wrong," Sam said, scratching the top of Ginger's head. "I was looking forward to meeting this little girl. But I wouldn't have thought of bringing her a Christmas gift."

"I guess running a growing non-profit wouldn't leave you much time for buying presents for your four-legged friends," Zach said.

When Sam stood and looked up, the sight of the Gulf of Mexico through the double sliding doors in Connie's living room stopped him in his tracks. "Wow, kiddo, what a view!" He slowly walked over to the sliders, while Ginger sat in the corner and went to town on her new chew toy.

"I can see why you moved here. This view is exquisite."

"The view is the same from the guest room," Connie said. "Why don't you settle in and relax? I'll put dinner in the oven."

Sam tugged at his fleece sweatshirt. "I need to get out of these winter clothes and put on something more appropriate for Florida weather."

Zach showed Sam to Connie's guest suite, where she had already pulled down the Murphy bed and put fresh sheets on it. All there was for Sam to do was unpack.

While Sam settled in, Connie put some breaded chicken breasts into the oven and heated up some mashed potatoes, which she had also prepared earlier. Then she sauteed some string beans in olive oil, garlic, and spices while Zach set the table.

About fifteen minutes later, Sam emerged from his room wearing summer khakis and a short-sleeved blue and white button-down shirt. "This is much better," he said with a satisfied smile.

Before they sat down to eat, Connie made a quick phone call to check in with Abby, her employee who was covering the store so Connie could take the evening off. It was a late Friday afternoon in early January, which was one of the busiest months since the snowbirds and tourists were returning in full force, so Connie wanted to make sure Abby wasn't too overwhelmed.

"Everything is okay at the store," Connie said when she hung up with Abby. "But I don't like that Abby or Grace has to cover for me every time I want to take some time off. Although Abby insists she doesn't mind, because she is still on winter break and could use the extra money, it still feels like an imposition."

"Can you afford to hire another employee?" Sam asked, after they said the blessing together.

Connie put two cutlets on her plate. "I probably should. I've thought about it, but I just bought the building where my store is housed and took on a mortgage that was higher than my rent had been, so expenses have gone up. I'm afraid of taking on too much overhead. Besides, I want to expand the Fair Trade section of the store, and as I take on more vendors, that means more upfront costs."

"It sounds like you're a busy lady," Sam said. "Of course, that doesn't surprise me. Old habits die hard."

"Speaking of old habits, you must be slowing down a little bit," Connie said. "I can't believe you took off two entire weeks."

Sam let out a sigh.

"You don't seem very excited about it," Connie said. "Is everything okay?"

Sam shook his head, as if trying to shake off his thoughts. "Don't mind me. This vacation is just what the doctor ordered. I've been looking forward to it for months. I'm just tired."

"From work?" Connie asked.

"Probably from the last thirteen years in general. The truth is, initially I was only planning to come for a week, but Janet insisted that I extend my vacation. I've been tired for a long time."

Connie's eyes flew open. "Sam, you're not sick, are you?"

He shook his head. "No, it's nothing like that. I just had a physical, and my doctor said that everything looks great. I guess I've just been working too hard. Perhaps my age is catching up with me. Janet's probably right. I just need some time off."

"It sounds like you're burning out," Zach said. "We've all been there. An extended vacation could be just what you need."

"Thanks, Zach. I hope you're right."

After dinner, Sam offered to take Ginger for her nightly walk while Connie and Zach cleaned up.

"I think I'll turn in early and do some reading," Sam said when he returned and saw that the kitchen had been cleaned.

Sam retired to his room, and Connie accompanied Zach to the elevator.

"Something is different about Sam," Connie said after Zach pressed the elevator call button. "The Sam I know and love was a big ball of energy."

"I'm sure he'll be back to his old self after a few days of rest and relaxation - not to mention the warm Florida sunshine."

"I hope you're right. But I know Sam, and it looks to me like it will take more than a few days in the sun. I really wanted to hit the ground running and pick his brain about expanding my Fair Trade section while he was here, but now I'm afraid to bring up anything work-related. He looks so fragile."

"Maybe focusing on *your* work will help him to get his mind off his own. I'm sure he'd be happy to be your sounding board."

"You could be right. I guess I'll play it by ear."

When the elevator arrived, Zach kissed Connie and left.

Chapter 2

CONNIE HAD SET her phone alarm to wake up early on Saturday morning. After showering, she took Ginger for a long walk, and when she returned, Sam was still sleeping.

"Sam must really be tired," she said to Ginger as she unhooked the dog's leash. "Back in the day, Sam would already be in the office by now."

While Connie waited for Sam to wake up, she mixed some pancake batter and scrambled some eggs to make a 'Welcome to Sapphire Beach' breakfast for him. Within ten minutes of the batter hitting the pan, she heard stirring in the guest bedroom, followed by the sound of the shower running in the attached bathroom.

By the time Sam showered and dressed, Connie was just pulling the scrambled eggs from the frying pan and had placed a stack of pancakes on the table, along with some warm maple syrup and soft butter.

"My favorite breakfast," Sam said with a broad smile as he loaded his plate with pancakes and eggs and lathered everything with a healthy dose of syrup.

Connie laughed. "I guess your fatigue hasn't affected your appetite."

"I feel better already," he said. "I slept with the window open and left all my cares fifteen hundred miles away."

"That's the spirit," Connie said.

The dark circles remained beneath Sam's eyes and he wasn't yet back to his high-energy self, but Connie hoped a hearty breakfast would keep him moving in the right direction.

"If you're feeling up to it, I could show you *Just Jewelry* this morning, then we could visit the other shops that carry our Fair Trade products. I'm hoping to both expand the Fair Trade section in my own store, since the product is selling well, and to increase the number of vendors who carry merchandise created by our artisans." Connie poured herself another glass of milk. "So far, there are two: Ruby, who carries beach bags and other touristy items in her souvenir shop and Kate, who owns *Beach Baby Boutique*. She carries some children's accessories. I was hoping we could brainstorm together on some ways to grow and potentially expand my number of suppliers." At the moment, all of Connie's suppliers were in Kenya and Ecuador.

"Are you sure you want to expand?" Sam asked. "You probably earn less profit on Fair Trade jewelry than you do on the pieces you create yourself."

Connie thought she might have misunderstood Sam. That didn't sound like him.

"You know that it's not all about making money with the Fair Trade product. I do make a profit, but my main purpose is to empower communities and employ artisans so they can support their families."

"You're right," Sam said. "Of course. I just don't want to see you spread yourself too thin."

"You know me well," Connie said. "I'll be careful." She glanced at Sam. "If you'd rather spend the day on the beach, I can join you later on."

"Are you kidding? I can't wait to see *Just Jewelry*. I'll have plenty of time in the next couple of weeks to enjoy the sand and the surf."

As soon as they loaded the dishwasher with their breakfast dishes, they took Ginger and drove the mile-long commute down Sapphire Beach Boulevard to the downtown area. Between Sam's present the night before and all the attention he had been lavishing on her, Sam had made an enthusiastic little friend.

By the time they arrived, Grace was about to open the store.

Connie introduced Sam and Grace, and they sat down to enjoy a cup of coffee Grace had brewed. It warmed Connie's heart to see two people who meant so much to her finally in the same room. Sam was a true extrovert who loved meeting new people, so Connie wasn't surprised that he and Grace talked as if they were old friends.

About a half hour after they opened, a customer came into the store. Grace helped her find what she was looking for, while Connie gave Sam the grand tour.

"You've done a fantastic job, Connie," Sam said. "It's even more beautiful than I imagined."

"I owe so much to your support and guidance over the years," Connie said. "If you hadn't trusted me with so many aspects of your non-profit, I wouldn't have had the confidence or connections to make this work, especially with my Ecuadorian suppliers. Like I told Zach, our friendship has always been such a blessing in my life."

"You never know where life is going to lead," Grace said, who had rejoined them after ringing up the customer's purchase. "Who would have known when I became friends with Concetta so many years ago that one day her niece would be such an important part of my life?"

Connie smiled at her friend, neighbor, and employee. "The feeling is mutual."

"Listen, you two don't have to hang around here," Grace said. "Why don't you show Sam around Sapphire Beach on his first day in town?"

"I was hoping to give Sam a tour of the downtown area. I especially wanted to show him the two shops that carry our Fair Trade products. Maybe

I'll do that now so I can be back before the afternoon rush."

First, Connie took Sam next door to Ruby's souvenir shop, and introduced him to Ruby. Next, they stopped by *Beach Baby Boutique* but decided to return later, since the owner, Kate, wouldn't be in until the afternoon. After strolling up and down the downtown streets, they ended up at a bench by the pier.

"I don't want to keep you from the store on a busy Saturday," Sam said. "I can entertain myself for the afternoon."

"Why don't you take my car for a while?" Connie offered. "If you come back later this afternoon, we can stop in and visit Kate. Grace and Abby are working extra hours tomorrow, so I can take most of the day off. We can do something fun then."

"That sounds perfect." He nodded toward the crystal blue water and white sand. "The beach is calling my name, so I think I'll soak up some sun."

Connie was glad that she didn't leave Grace alone for too long, because it turned out to be a crazy-busy afternoon. The snowbirds and tourists were back in full force. They made so many sales that by the end of the afternoon, Connie had to replenish some of the merchandise from her storage room out back.

Grace left at 2:00, as usual, and Connie was on her own until Abby arrived at 4:00. She really should consider hiring additional help, at least for the busy months.

Just as things started to slow down, Sam returned. His cheeks were pink from the sun and he already looked a bit more like his old self.

"An afternoon at the beach was just what I needed," Sam said. "I feel better already."

After introducing Sam and Abby, Connie and Sam headed over to *Beach Baby Boutique* in hopes of catching Kate.

Fortunately, they found her hanging designer children's clothes when they arrived.

Connie introduced Sam and Kate, and Kate showed Sam the Fair Trade children's jewelry, pocketbooks, and backpacks that were popular in her store. "When someone purchases a Fair Trade item for a child, we always provide information on the artisan and their home country as an educational component. Both the children and parents love it."

"Without Sam's support, I doubt I would have opened my store," Connie said. "He is the founder of the non-profit I worked at for eleven years."

"Then I guess I have you to thank, as well as Connie, for my success with Fair Trade merchandise," Kate said.

As they were talking, a man walked into the store and gave Kate a curt wave.

"Get over here, Jeffrey Collins!" Kate said. "When did you get that haircut?"

Jeff skimmed his hand over his apparently new crew cut.

"My brother has been wearing his hair almost to his shoulders for as long as I can remember," Kate explained.

"Since I'm turning thirty-five in a few weeks, I broke down and got a grown-up haircut. Besides, I got tired of my friends' teasing. They always say that my long hair makes me look like one of the teenagers in our program."

"It looks good, little brother," Kate said. "By the way, this is Connie, the one who supplies the Fair

Trade items that I've been carrying. And this is her friend, Sam. Sam founded a non-profit in the Boston area."

Jeff extended his hand. "It's great to meet you. I was so happy to hear that Kate started carrying Fair Trade."

"Jeff is also in non-profit work," Kate said to Sam. "He is the founder of Sapphire Beach's only after-school program."

"That sounds like wonderful work," Sam said.

"I only started it a couple of years ago, so it's relatively new. Say, Sam, if you have any time while you're in town, I'd love to pick your brain. Maybe we could have coffee or lunch."

"Absolutely," Sam said. "Are you available now? Connie has to get back to her shop for a few more hours, so I'm free for dinner."

Connie had to smile. Sam had a knack for making friends faster than anyone she knew.

"I'd love that," Jeff said. "My wife met with an old friend from high school for coffee this afternoon and then she was planning to do some shopping, so I'm a bachelor at the moment. How about if I take you to

Gallagher's Tropical Shack? It's one of my favorite places to grab dinner."

"That's perfect," Connie said. "*Gallagher's* is right across the street from my shop. You can meet me at the store when you're done and by that time, I should be ready to leave."

"Great. I'll see you a little later," Sam said as he left with Jeff.

Connie returned to *Just Jewelry* just in time for a late afternoon rush. By the time she saw Sam walking across the street from *Gallagher's* a couple of hours later, the foot traffic had cleared out.

"How was dinner?" Connie asked.

Sam grinned. "Jeff is a character. I enjoyed talking with him. We talked shop for most of the night, and I gave him my best advice on expanding the mission of his non-profit, which is his goal. He was soaking in everything I said like a sponge. He reminds me of myself when I was first starting off."

"In that case, I'm so happy we ran into him."

Sam appeared more energized. Perhaps sharing his experience, in addition to some beach time, had given him a needed boost of energy.

Abby peered out the large display window at the front of the shop. "The downtown streets are clearing out, so I don't think we'll be getting many more customers. Why don't the two of you call it an early night?"

"Thanks, Abby. I think we might."

Connie attached Ginger's leash, and she, Sam, and Ginger headed back to Palm Paradise. They took Ginger for a walk before going upstairs. Connie heated up some leftovers for herself, since Sam had already eaten. They chatted for a while, then decided to call it an early night. They needed to wake up early for Mass the following morning.

Just as Connie was dozing off, she heard the ping of a text. She groggily reached for her phone.

The message was from Zach.

Sorry to text so late, but I'm downstairs and I need to talk to you and Sam.

Now? Connie replied. *Is everything okay?*

Not exactly. This isn't a social call. It's police business.

I'll buzz you in.

Within five minutes, Zach was sitting at the dining room table across from Connie and Sam.

"I hate to be the bearer of bad news, but Jeff Collins was found dead in his car on the side of the road tonight, and I understand Sam was one of the last people to see him alive."

Now, Connie was fully awake.

Chapter 3

THE COLOR THAT HAD JUST begun to return to Sam's cheeks drained away in seconds.

"There must be some mistake, Zach," Sam said. "I only met Jeff once, but he appeared to be in perfect health."

"He very well might have been. The medical examiner thinks he died from carbon monoxide poisoning," Zach said.

Sam's mouth fell open.

"I don't understand," Connie said. "You need to be in an enclosed area for that to happen. You said his body was discovered in his car on the side of the road."

"That's right," Zach said. "That's why we think someone killed him in another location, then dumped his car with his body inside. If Jeff's death had been an accident, he would have been found in a garage or some other confined space."

Sam stared blankly in Zach's direction. "I just can't believe it." He glanced at the time on Connie's microwave, which was visible from his seat at the dining room table. "Jeff and I were eating dinner together at *Gallagher's* just six hours ago. He shared with me his hopes and dreams for the after-school program he recently founded. Why would anyone kill him? Are you sure it was the same Jeff Collins?"

"I'm afraid it's not a mistake," Zach said. "I wish it were. He was only thirty-four years old, but Jeff was quickly becoming a pillar of the community. Those kids are going to miss him. It's an incalculable loss for Sapphire Beach."

"Poor Kate," Connie said.

"I just finished talking with her. She was heading to Jeff's house so she could be with his wife, Rachel, and the rest of the family.

"Did Jeff have any children?" Connie asked.

Sam shook his head. "No. Jeff told me that he and his wife had been unable to have children. That was partly what inspired him to leave his position in social work to start the after-school program. He said he loved those kids as if they were his own."

Connie could relate. She didn't have any children of her own yet, either, and at thirty-six years old, she didn't know if she ever would. The children she served throughout her years in Africa, and later with *Feeding the Hungry,* held a special place in her own heart, as well. And not having a family of her own left her with more time and energy to devote to her work of serving other families. Perhaps that was one of the reasons she was so eager to expand her Fair Trade business.

"Sam, I know you only met Jeff once, but you were one of the last people to see him alive," Zach said. "Think back over your conversation with him. Did he say or do anything that might indicate that he felt he was in danger?"

Sam sighed and leaned his elbows on the table. Then he shook his head. "I can't think of a single thing. We mostly talked shop. He was interested in hearing how we took *Feeding the Hungry* from a small operation to the organization it is today. He had big dreams for the after-school program, which included an expansion to offer additional services to the community. He told me that he received his Master's degree in Social Work, and after getting his license, he worked as a case manager for several years. But he quickly realized that so many kids needed a more consistent positive presence in their lives. That was why he founded the program. That was the gist of what we talked about, Zach. I'm sorry I can't be of more help, but there was nothing suspicious about anything he said."

"Okay," Zach said. "If anything comes to you, give me a call."

"Will do."

Zach stood to leave, and Connie followed him to the door. "Please keep us posted on the case. I hope you are able to bring his killer to justice, both for his family's sake and for the children he would have spent the rest of his life serving."

Zach took Connie's hand and squeezed it. "We will do our best."

After he left, Connie rejoined Sam at the dining room table. He was staring blankly at the wall.

"I think I'm in shock," he said when Connie sat down.

"I'm so sorry this happened during your visit. I was hoping your time in Sapphire Beach would be refreshing, not bring you sadness."

"Don't be silly," Sam said. "I feel honored to have met Jeff. Besides, you know me. I believe everything happens for a reason, even if we don't understand why. I think I was meant to meet Jeff. His passion reminded me of why I do what I do."

"I can't imagine that any of your passion has waned," Connie said.

A melancholy look came across Sam's face.

"What is it?" Connie asked.

Sam's gaze dropped to the ground. "Nothing. I'm just tired, that's all."

"Why don't we get some sleep? We have to be up for the early Mass tomorrow," Connie said, glancing at the time. It was nearly midnight. "On second thought, why don't you go with Grace to the 9:00 Mass? You can catch a ride with her to the store afterwards."

Sam gave Connie a tired smile. "I might just do that. A couple of extra hours sleep sounds good about now."

Since it was late, and Connie didn't want to wake Grace with a text, she walked next door and slipped a note under Grace's door asking her to come over to pick up Sam before Mass.

"All set," Connie said when she returned. "The church is only five minutes away, so she'll probably pick you up about 8:45."

"Maybe after Mass you and I could pay Kate a visit to offer our condolences," Sam suggested.

"That's a good idea. We can stop by *Beach Baby Boutique* to get Kate's home address."

Connie tossed and turned all night, so she was barely asleep when her alarm went off less than six hours later. She took a quick shower and made herself an English muffin and a mug of tea. Then she took Ginger for a walk and headed to Mass.

After Mass, Connie stopped by her condo to pick up Ginger before heading downtown.

Sunday mornings were generally quiet, since many tourists and residents either hadn't yet ventured out or were at church. When Grace and Sam arrived at *Just Jewelry* at 10:15 with three coffees in hand, Connie had just finished helping one of the only customers who had come in the store so far.

"Sam told me what happened to Kate's brother," Grace said, handing Connie one of the coffees. "How awful. Please give Kate my deepest sympathy when you see her."

"We will," Connie said. "We wanted to offer our condolences this morning. Abby is coming in at noon today so I can spend some time with Sam. If you don't mind, I think we'll go now. Tell Abby I will be back before you leave for the day."

"Go. Sunday mornings are slow, even in January. I can handle things alone until Abby arrives."

Connie and Sam walked to *Beach Baby Boutique*, hoping that Kate's employees would know where they could find Kate. However, to their surprise, Kate was there. She looked as though she was barely keeping it together. When she saw Connie and Sam, she came right over.

"We just had to come and offer our condolences," Sam said. "We're so sorry about Jeff."

Kate wiped the tears from her eyes with a tissue she had been holding, then motioned for them to follow her into her office at the back of the store.

"Thank you for coming," Kate said, losing her battle to fight back the tears. "I feel completely lost. It feels as though I'm functioning on autopilot. I just came to the store to personally deliver the news of Jeff's death to my employees and to make sure the store has coverage for the next few days, since I obviously won't be coming in. They are, of course, being wonderful and assured me they would take care of everything in my absence."

"The police said that it appears as if Jeff's death wasn't an accident," Connie said. "Zach came by last night to talk with Sam, since he was one of the last people to see Jeff alive."

"Did you notice anything that could help the police?" Kate asked.

Sam shook his head. "Nothing at all. We talked about his plans for the after-school program, and he asked me a lot of questions about my own non-profit. He seemed like a remarkable young man," Sam said. "I'm so sorry this happened."

"Thank you. He was." Kate's gaze dropped toward the floor, then she suddenly looked up at Connie. "Haven't you helped the police solve a lot of murders in town? I remember you coming by one time to ask me questions about a suspect in another investigation."

"That's right," Sam said. "I almost forgot. Connie's parents tell me that she seems to have developed a hobby for solving crimes since moving to Sapphire Beach."

Kate gripped Connie's hand. "Could you ask around and see what you can find out? I know it's asking a lot, especially during this busy season and with an out-of-town guest. I wouldn't ask if it weren't my brother."

Connie hesitated. It wasn't that she minded getting involved, but her plate was full at the moment.

"I think you should," Sam said. "And even though everyone is trying to get me to take it easy, I can only spend so much time sitting still. I could be your sidekick. As one of the last people to see Jeff alive and being kindred spirits of sorts, it's the least I can do."

"Well, since you put it that way," Connie said, "I suppose we could try. But you'd have to help us, Kate. I have no idea where we would even start. We don't know anything about Jeff."

"Absolutely. I'll tell you anything you want to know."

"Let's start with his wife," Connie said. "How was their marriage?"

"Rachel? Oh, she's a sweetheart. She couldn't have had anything to do with Jeff's death. I was with her last night. She is devastated."

"So, there wasn't any sort of large insurance policy or anything like that?" Connie asked.

"No. In fact, we talked about that last night. Jeff had just enough life insurance to cover his funeral expenses. In fact, his death puts Rachel in a worse place financially. She might even have to sell their home without Jeff's income."

"Is there anyone else you can think of who might want to harm Jeff? Or any suspicious behavior?"

Kate's jaw dropped.

"What is it?" Sam asked.

"I wouldn't have thought anything of it, but given the circumstances... No, they are best friends. He couldn't have."

"Who are you talking about?" Connie asked.

"Trevor Hines. He and Jeff were old college roommates, and they both went on to get their

Master's degrees in Social Work together. Trevor is a case manager for the State of Florida now, like Jeff used to be, and was very supportive of Jeff's after-school program."

"It doesn't sound like Trevor had any motive to kill Jeff," Connie said. "What made you think of him?"

"Trevor and Jeff had some type of falling out a few months ago. Jeff refused to tell me what it was all about. I ran into Trevor recently and asked him about it, but he was as tight-lipped as Jeff was. Something happened between the two of them, but neither of them would talk about it."

"Do you think Rachel would know what happened?" Connie asked.

"I don't know, but we could try asking her. I'm headed to her house now. Would you like to come?"

Connie looked at Sam, who nodded.

"We'd love to."

Chapter 4

CONNIE AND SAM RETRIEVED Connie's car in the parking lot near *Just Jewelry* and followed Kate to a small house on the edge of town. Kate knocked on the front door but walked in without waiting for anyone to answer.

"I'm not alone!" Kate yelled into the house. "I brought a couple of friends."

"I'm in here!" came a woman's voice from a nearby room.

Kate led Connie and Sam into the living room where they found a woman with short, dark, wavy hair and pensive brown eyes sitting on an armchair.

"Please tell me you haven't been alone all morning," Kate said.

"No," Rachel replied. "My parents were here, but they just left to do some grocery shopping."

Kate breathed a sigh of relief. "Thank goodness. Rachel, these are my friends, Connie and Sam. This is Rachel, Jeff's wife."

Connie extended her hand, and Rachel shook it without getting up.

"We're so sorry for your loss," Connie said. "I can't imagine what you must be going through."

She gave them a half smile.

"How are you doing today?" Kate asked.

Rachel shrugged her shoulders. "You know..." Her voice trailed off.

"I brought Connie and Sam over, because I thought they might be able to help us find out what happened to Jeff."

Rachel knit her brow. "Are they with the police?"

"No," Kate said. "But Connie has a knack for solving tough crimes. She's helped the police on many occasions. And Sam is the man Jeff had dinner with last night."

"Oh, yes, of course. I remember. You founded some type of non-profit up north. Jeff came home all enthusiastic. I was exhausted, so he waited to tell

38

me about your conversation until today. But he never got the chance."

"He was quite the young man," Sam said. "He knew how to dream big."

"He certainly did," Rachel said. "I loved that about him."

Connie, Sam, and Kate sat on the sofa across from Rachel.

"I know it's a difficult time for you," Connie said, "but we were hoping you could tell us more about Jeff."

"What would you like to know?" Rachel asked.

"Did he have any enemies?"

"Jeff wasn't the type to have enemies," Rachel said. "He was just the opposite, actually. He had a way with people, especially children and teens. For as long as I've known him, he never got into trouble. This just doesn't make any sense."

"Do you know if Jeff came home after he and I had dinner?" Sam asked.

"Yes," Rachel said. "As I told the police, I had coffee with a high school friend yesterday afternoon, and then I did some shopping. We both got home about the same time." She smiled. "He was dying to see what I would think of his haircut, and I teased him that since he looked older now, I'd need to find a younger guy. We sat down to watch a movie, but shortly after it started, he said that he got a text and he had to run out for a little while."

"Was that unusual?" Connie asked.

"It was rare, but not so unusual that I thought anything of it. Once in a while, a teenager would call him if he or she were in some sort of trouble or needed to talk. Some of the teens at his after-school program had difficult home lives. They didn't have anyone else to turn to. I asked him if he wanted me to come with him, and he said it wasn't necessary. I thought that was strange, because he would never meet a teen alone. It's always a good idea to have another adult present. But I figured maybe Tim was joining him. Tim is a teacher who works with Jeff in the after-school program."

"So, you have no idea who he was meeting?" Connie asked.

Rachel shook her head. "The strange thing is that the police checked Jeff's phone and said that there was no text."

"Jeff made it up?" Connie asked.

"Apparently. The police are going to question all the kids Jeff worked with to see if he was supposed to meet any of them. But he definitely said he received a text, so it sounds like he just used it as an excuse. I have no idea why."

"Kate mentioned that the relationship between Jeff and his friend, Trevor, was strained. Do you know anything about that?"

Rachel looked at Kate. "I have no idea. It was the strangest thing. Something happened between the two of them, but Jeff was always so evasive when I would ask him about it."

"How do you mean?" Connie asked.

"Well, they were so close for so long and then, out of the blue, Trevor stopped coming around. I asked Jeff about it several times, but he never gave me a straight answer."

"Did Jeff seem angry about it?" Connie asked.

"He seemed more disappointed. I asked him directly if they had had a falling out, and he said they hadn't. He even defended Trevor, saying he was a great guy, and I should never think otherwise, but they just needed some space in their relationship."

"Jeff wouldn't tell me what happened, either," Kate said. "I ran into Trevor at Publix last month. He tried to avoid me, but I wouldn't let him. He said a quick hello and then made his excuses and left the store. He even left behind a cart full of groceries that he had apparently intended to purchase. I told Jeff, and he just said Trevor was going through some stuff and not to worry about it."

As they were talking with Rachel, the doorbell rang.

Kate jumped up. "I'll get it."

When she returned, a man with light brown hair and hazel eyes was with her. He cautiously approached Rachel and put his arms around her.

"Speak of the devil," Kate whispered to Connie and Sam. "That's Trevor."

"I'm so sorry, Rachel. I just heard about Jeff. Do you know what happened?"

Rachel started to sob. "I have no idea, Trevor."

"I'm so sorry," he kept repeating.

Connie and Sam looked at one another, then back at Trevor. Connie wanted to ask Trevor about what happened between him and Jeff, but it clearly wasn't the right moment.

"I don't know what to say," Trevor continued.

"Thank you for coming. You were his closest friend," Rachel said.

Rachel motioned for Trevor to sit down, and it was only then that he noticed Connie and Sam.

"Trevor, Connie and Sam are friends of mine," Kate said. "I've asked them to help us look into what happened to Jeff."

Trevor's eyes flew open. "What do you mean? Aren't the police investigating?"

"They are, but Connie is a gifted amateur sleuth and I thought it couldn't hurt to have her and Sam checking things out, as well. Sam was one of the last people to see Jeff alive."

Trevor cleared his throat. "That doesn't sound like a good idea to me. I think you should let the police handle it. You don't want to walk into a dangerous situation."

Connie studied Trevor's eyes. Was that fear?

"I hadn't thought of that," Kate said.

"Don't worry. We'll be careful," Connie assured her.

Rachel turned her attention back to Trevor. "It's so good to see you again, Trevor. It's been a long time. Several months, at least."

Trevor, who had sat down next to Connie and Sam, squirmed in his seat. "I know I haven't been around much, but Jeff and I just needed a little time apart. We would have been fine."

Kate looked at Connie and Sam and shrugged in frustration.

"Jeff wouldn't tell me what the problem was, either," Rachel said.

"That's because it was no big deal," Trevor said, squeezing Rachel's forearm. "He was telling the truth."

"Well, we've taken up enough of your time," Connie said. "We should get going."

Connie took a business card from her wallet and handed it to Rachel. "If you remember anything, please call me."

Trevor glanced at his wristwatch. "I should be going, too. Justine went to Immokalee this weekend with her sisters, and she'll be home any minute. They stayed at the casino hotel last night, so she still doesn't know what happened to Jeff. She's going to be devastated. My wife was very fond of Jeff." Trevor stood to leave. "If there's anything we can do, please don't hesitate to reach out. I'm sure Justine will be calling you later."

Connie, Sam, and Trevor walked out at the same time and went in the same direction. Connie assumed it was Trevor's Honda Civic parked behind her silver Jetta.

When they arrived at their cars, Trevor paused before getting in. "I'm sure you're wondering, so I'll just tell you right off. I was home alone last night, so I don't have an alibi for when Jeff was killed. But he was my best friend. I never would have hurt him."

"Do you have any idea who did?" Connie asked.

"I didn't want to say it in front of Rachel, but she's right that Jeff and I had a disagreement. Jeff was spending too much time at the home of a woman — a single woman named Kelly. I told him it was inappropriate, but he wouldn't listen. He said he was helping her with some household repairs, but if you ask me, there was more to it than that. If I were you, I would pay a visit to Kelly Robinson and ask her what she knows about Jeff's death."

"Are you saying that Jeff and Kelly were having an affair?" Sam asked.

"Why else would he go to her house on his lunch break three days a week? You should look into it. She lives at 26 Seagull Lane."

Before Connie could say anything, Trevor disappeared into his car.

Chapter 5

WHILE CONNIE AND SAM were driving back to *Just Jewelry* from Rachel's house, Connie's cell phone rang. She took it out of her purse and glanced at the screen.

It was Elyse.

Connie handed it to Sam, who transferred the call to speaker mode.

"Hi Elyse, you're on speaker. I'm in my car with Sam."

Elyse breathed a loud sigh of relief. "Thank goodness I caught you." She sounded as if she were trying to catch her breath.

"Is everything all right?" Connie asked. "You sound winded."

"No. I mean - I don't know." Elyse took a deep breath. "It's Gertrude."

Connie's heart felt as if it dropped to her feet.

Gertrude was Elyse's great-aunt and one of Connie's favorite residents of Palm Paradise.

"What happened to Gertrude?"

"I don't know the details yet," Elyse said. "My parents just called to let me know that Gertrude was taken to the emergency room. They are on their way to the hospital now. Apparently, Gertrude got lightheaded and complained of burning in her chest while she was sitting in the lobby of Palm Paradise. One of the other residents called 9-1-1 just to be on the safe side. Connie, it sounds like she could have had a heart attack. I really want to go to her, but Josh is working on the investigation, and I'd rather not take Emma and Victoria to the hospital. I know it's a lot to ask on a busy Sunday, but I was wondering if I could leave the girls with you at *Just Jewelry*."

Emma was Elyse's and Josh's thirteen-year-old daughter, and Victoria was their five-year-old.

"Of course," Connie said. "Sam and I are driving back to the store. We're only about five minutes away."

Elyse and the girls arrived at *Just Jewelry* a few minutes after Connie and Sam. Connie hugged Elyse as soon as she came through the door.

"Thank you so much," Elyse said. "The girls love being in your store, and I didn't know where else to take them."

Connie put her arm around both girls' shoulders. "It will be a good chance for us to spend some time together. Take as much time as you need. We'll be here all day, and if we go home early, we'll take the girls with us and you can pick them up at my place."

After Grace finished helping a customer, she came over. "Keep us posted on Gertrude. We'll say some prayers."

"Thank you. I appreciate that."

Grace squeezed Elyse's shoulder. "Don't worry. Gertrude is as tough as they come. She's going to be fine."

But Elyse didn't appear convinced.

The store was beginning to get busy. Even though Emma helped in the shop from time to time, she decided to spend the day making a get-well gift for Gertrude. So, Connie set her up with everything she needed to make a green and blue beaded bracelet. Emma had taken several of Connie's jewelry-making classes, and she was becoming quite the expert.

Sam entertained Victoria with some coloring books Elyse had brought, while Connie and Grace attended to customers.

At noon, Abby arrived. She looked surprised when she saw Emma, Victoria, Sam, Connie, and Grace all in the store. "Wow. You have a full house today. I thought if I came in early you might take the day off to show Sam around."

"That will have to wait for now," Connie said. She and Sam caught Abby up both on Jeff's death and the situation with Gertrude.

"In that case, it's a good thing I'm here," Abby said. "It sounds like you could use an extra hand."

While Grace tended to customers, Abby supervised Victoria, giving Connie and Sam a chance to discuss their conversations with Rachel and Trevor.

"There's something about Trevor that I don't trust," Connie said. "And he doesn't have an alibi.

He was home alone last night while his wife was in Immokalee."

Sam nodded in agreement. "We need to talk with Kelly Robinson. I doubt she'd admit to having an affair with Jeff, but at least we might be able to gage her reaction."

"Trevor gave us Kelly's address, so I suppose we could drop in and ask her some questions. But we need to wait until Elyse comes back to get the girls."

"That sounds like a plan," Sam said. "How about if the girls and I take Ginger for a walk and pick us all up some sandwiches?"

Connie proposed Sam's plan to the girls, and they enthusiastically agreed.

"I'll take Ginger," Emma said, fastening the dog's leash.

"I guess it's settled then," Connie said.

Since Grace and Abby were both in the store, Connie did some paperwork until Sam and the girls returned about forty-five minutes later.

"We had a great little walk," Sam said. "We weaved our way through all the side streets. Your dog is quite popular. At every turn, shop employees came out to say hello to her."

Connie bent down and scratched the fur on the top of Ginger's head. "Oh, she's a little ham."

Connie, Grace, and Abby rotated between eating, entertaining Victoria, and assisting customers until Grace left at 2:00.

Sam proved to be a great helper. Since he personally knew Connie's Fair Trade artisans, he made himself useful talking to customers about the artisans and life in the villages where they were from.

"I should give you a commission," Connie said.

"I'm happy to see those pieces move. There is a lot of potential here. I can see why you want to expand your Fair Trade section. Just be sure that you are not taking on too much. You have a lot on your plate right now, including your relationship with Zach. Don't forget to stop and enjoy this time with him."

At the mention of Zach's name, Connie couldn't help but smile. "I never had the chance to ask you what you thought of him."

"From what I saw, he seems like exactly the kind of man you should be with. Of course, I only met him once, if you don't count the night he came over to tell us about Jeff."

"Let's fix that," Connie said. "I really want you and Zach to get to know each other better. I'll text him and see if he is free to join us for a late dinner tonight. If Josh is working today, Zach probably is, too, but maybe he can join us later on."

Sam nodded. "I'd like that."

While Connie was texting Zach, Elyse returned. She looked as if the weight of the world were on her shoulders.

The girls ran over to her, and Emma showed her the bracelet she made for Gertrude.

"It's lovely, honey. Aunt Gertrude will love it."

Sam entertained the girls for a few minutes so Connie and Elyse could talk.

"How is Gertrude?" Connie asked.

"She seems to be okay. They ran some tests, and it wasn't a heart attack. But they are going to hold her overnight for observation. They still don't know what happened."

"That sounds like good news," Connie said. "Maybe the neighbor who called 9-1-1 just over-reacted."

"I hope so," Elyse said, her eyes filling with tears.

"I know." Connie gave her friend a supportive hug. "It's scary."

"It's not just that. I haven't been getting over to see her nearly as much as I used to. We spent Christmas together, but the last couple of times she invited me over, I couldn't go. I'll never forgive myself if anything happens to her."

"I'm sure she understands that your life is busy. Between the girls and your real estate business, I don't know how you find time to do anything."

"I know, but what if it's too late?"

"You can't think like that," Connie said. "She's going to be fine, and you can make it a point to visit more frequently."

Elyse nodded. "I hope you're right."

It was nearly 5:00 when Elyse and the girls left. About a half hour later, the downtown streets began to empty out, and Connie and Sam decided to call it a day.

When Connie finally had a moment to check her phone, there was a reply from Zach. He was finishing up some work with Josh, then had a few other things to do, but he was hoping to be finished by 7:00 and would love to come over.

Perfect, Connie replied. *We'll see you when you get there.*

"We have enough time to stop by Kelly's if you're still up for it," Connie said. "Zach won't be coming over until after 7:00."

"Absolutely."

Connie tapped Kelly's address into her GPS, and fifteen minutes later, they had arrived.

"The lights are on, so it looks like someone is home," Sam said.

Connie parked in the street in front of the small beige house. They walked up the cement walkway, stepping over a couple of gaping cracks, and Connie noticed the paint was peeling in some sections.

She rang the doorbell.

A woman with long red hair who looked to be in her late twenties answered the door. Her eyes were bloodshot.

"If you're selling something, this isn't a good time," the woman said.

"Nothing like that. My name is Connie, and this is my friend, Sam. We're here on behalf of Kate Collins."

"Jeff's sister?" the woman asked.

"Yes," Sam said. "We're looking for Kelly Robinson."

She narrowed her eyes. "That's me."

A little boy with the same red hair as Kelly and a face full of freckles walked up timidly behind her.

"This is my son, Andy," she said, ruffling his hair.

"We were hoping we could talk to you for a few minutes about Jeff," Connie said.

Kelly opened the door wider to allow them to enter. "Andy, why don't you go play in your room for a few minutes?"

The boy took off, disappearing behind a white door at the end of a corridor, and Kelly motioned for Sam and Connie to sit at the kitchen table.

"I don't know how I could possibly help you, but Jeff was good to Andy and me, so I'm happy to answer any questions I can."

"We appreciate that," Connie said. "We heard that you and Jeff were close."

"I wouldn't exactly put it that way. But Jeff was a good friend when I needed one the most."

"We heard that you were..." Connie hesitated. "I might as well just say it. We heard that you and Jeff were more than friends."

Kelly's jaw fell. "What do you mean by that?"

"We heard that Jeff had been spending his lunch break at your house several days a week while your son was at school."

Kelly nodded. "He did. But it was nothing like what you seem to be implying. Andy attends Jeff's after-school program, and he told Jeff about my recent separation from my husband. Jeff knew I was working several jobs to make ends meet, so he offered to help out with some repairs around the house. With the loss of my husband's income because of our separation, I couldn't afford to make the repairs that the house needed, and still pay the rent."

"Aren't repairs your landlord's responsibility?" Connie asked.

"They should be, but so far he hasn't lifted a finger to help us. We're getting a good deal on the rent, so I didn't want to rock the boat. When Jeff offered to help me out on his lunch break, I gratefully accepted his offer. He wasn't a carpenter, but he was handy. Jeff was kind to Andy and me, but I assure you, it stopped there. My husband and I only separated a few months ago, so even if I would consider dating a married man - which I wouldn't - I'm not even ready for a relationship. All I have time to do is work and take care of Andy. Honestly, I don't know what we are going to do without Jeff's assistance."

"We just have one more question," Connie said. "Where were you on Saturday evening?"

"You mean, when Jeff was killed?"

Connie nodded.

"Andy was at a sleepover, so I was home alone. Stewart was supposed to take Andy that night, but he got the flu. My neighbor, who has a son Andy's age, knows that Saturday evenings are my only chance to relax, so she offered to take Andy."

Just then, Andy came out from his room. "Mom, can I have some juice?"

"We should let you go," Sam said. "Thank you for taking the time to talk to us."

"You're welcome. I hope you can figure out what happened to Jeff. His family deserves justice."

While Connie and Sam were driving back to Palm Paradise, Sam wondered aloud if Kelly was telling the truth.

"She did make a valid point," Connie said. "Between working and taking care of her son, it doesn't seem like she would have time for a relationship."

"You may be right, but you never can tell," Sam said. "As much as I don't want to believe that Jeff was having an affair, I don't think we can eliminate Kelly as a suspect."

Chapter 6

ON THEIR WAY HOME from Kelly's, Connie and Sam stopped at Publix to pick up the ingredients for Connie's famous Chicken Cordon Bleu with mashed potatoes and mixed vegetables.

Zach arrived shortly after 7:00 with a bottle of Pinot Grigio. He smiled when he saw Connie. "You are a sight for sore eyes. After a long day of interviews, it was nice to have something to look forward to tonight."

Sam and Zach enjoyed a glass of wine while Connie steamed the veggies. Since Sam and Zach were chatting away and getting to know each other, she took a little more time than was necessary preparing dinner.

When everything was ready, they sat at the dining room table and said the blessing together.

Connie and Sam recounted several stories from the years when they worked together. Connie was thrilled to be able to share that part of her life with Zach, since they had been such formative years.

Not to mention, Sam told a great story.

"Do you remember right after I hired you when we went to Ecuador to tour one of our partner organizations and missed our flight home?" Sam asked.

Connie laughed, nearly choking on the wine she had just sipped. "The phone lines at the hotel were down and we couldn't get through to my parents or Janet. They all showed up at Logan Airport expecting to pick us up and were horrified when we didn't get off the plane."

"Meanwhile, we were enjoying a great meal at a hotel near the airport, sharing a bottle of wine and participating in a lively sing-along at the bar."

"Both of our families forbade us to travel for nearly a year, and we both had to be on our best behavior in order to get back into their good graces."

Zach laughed. "You certainly kept your families on their toes."

"Poor Janet," Sam said. "I'm blessed to have an amazing wife who was willing to downsize our home and come with me on this ride. Without her support, *Feeding the Hungry* wouldn't exist."

"Sam's right about Janet," Connie said. "She's awesome. I'm sure you'll meet her someday."

"For sure," Sam said. "She wanted to come this time, but she was too busy at work."

After they finished dinner and cleared the table, Connie brought out a lemon cake and some vanilla ice cream.

"If I eat like this for the next two weeks, I'll need two seats on the return flight," Sam said.

"Actually, you look like you've lost weight," Connie said. "Consider this fair warning. I'll be doing my best to fatten you up before I send you home."

Sam stood and gave himself a once-over in the mirror, which hung on a wall on the other side of the dining area. "Maybe a little. I guess the stress is beginning to get to me."

"Can't you hire more help?" Zach asked.

Sam sipped his wine and looked pensively at Zach. "Probably. The organization continues to grow, which is good, but it means I've become more of a manager. I miss getting my hands dirty, like in the old days." Sam shook his head. "Anyway, enough about my woes. How is your investigation coming along? Are you any closer to figuring out what happened to Jeff?"

"It's only been twenty-four hours, so we're obviously still in the preliminary stages of interviewing. That will take a while. It's a time-consuming process."

"We reached out to Kate this morning to offer our condolences, and she told us that one of the children in Jeff's after-school program texted him on Saturday night, and that's why he went back out after having dinner with Sam." Connie didn't want to admit that Kate had taken them to Rachel's house to talk with her, so she kept her comment vague.

"That's what Jeff's wife told us, but there was no text on Jeff's phone that came through at that time. Also, we've spoken with all the kids in Jeff's program and none of them contacted Jeff last night."

"Are you sure the kids were telling the truth?" Connie asked.

Zach nodded. "We verified all of their alibis. They were either with friends or family. There's no way any of them met with Jeff last night."

So, Rachel was right. Something else caused Jeff to leave his house last night.

"I don't envy you your task," Sam said. "It sounds like you have a lot of tedious work ahead of you."

At 9:00, Zach decided to head home. "It's going to be a long week. I should get a good night's sleep."

Connie fastened Ginger's leash so she could bring her for a walk, then accompanied Zach downstairs. By the time she returned, the dishwasher was running, the dining room table was clean, and Sam was relaxing on the living room couch gazing into the darkness that covered the Gulf of Mexico. Sam had opened the sliders, and a cool breeze was drifting through her condo. It was an unseasonably warm evening for January.

Sam leaned back on Connie's baby blue tufted sofa. "The sound of the waves is lowering my blood pressure."

Connie sat in her favorite armchair, which faced the sliders. "I hate to see you so stressed out. You used to draw energy from your work, but now it seems to have the opposite effect. Do you think it might be time to retire?"

Sam thought for a moment. "I don't think that's the answer. You know me. I need to keep busy. What would I do with all that time on my hands? I'm only in my mid-fifties, and I have a lot of energy left. But Janet is considering retiring early and devoting more time to *Feeding the Hungry*."

"What about handing over the reins to someone else and transitioning to a smaller role? You could hire a manager and only do the things you enjoy."

"That's a thought. I just don't know if I'm quite ready for that. Besides, I don't know who I would hire. There's nobody I trust enough at this point."

Connie felt a twinge of guilt for having left *Feeding the Hungry* to move to Sapphire Beach. She knew Sam had been hoping that she would one day take over, since she had been part of the organization practically since its inception.

Sam must have read her mind. "I didn't mean it like that, Connie. You are clearly meant to be here in

Sapphire Beach, and I am so proud of the work you are doing with *Just Jewelry*. As I've said before, if *Feeding the Hungry* is my child, then that makes *Just Jewelry* my grandchild, and I'm a proud grandpa. Your shop is a fruit of the work we did together."

"I feel the same way," Connie said. "If it weren't for everything that I learned working for you, and if you hadn't entrusted me with so much responsibility, I doubt I would have had the confidence or experience to strike out on my own. I was involved in every aspect of the organization in the early days, and that prepared me for running a business."

"You and Zach are right about one thing," Sam said. "Even in just the short time I've been here, I can see that I need to make some sort of change. Now that I've put some distance between me and *Feeding the Hungry*, not to mention a couple of good nights' sleep, I'm gaining a fresh perspective. I'm going to give it a lot of thought in the next couple of weeks."

"I'm glad to hear that," Connie said.

"And speaking of problems to solve, we need to figure out our next move regarding the investigation."

"I was thinking about that while I was walking Ginger," Connie said. "Maybe we should talk to Kate and see if she has any ideas."

"Won't she be busy with the wake and funeral?" Sam asked.

"Good point." Connie pulled her laptop out from its carrying case and brought it into the living room. She did an Internet search for Jeff Collins and pulled up his obituary. "Jeff's wake is at 9:00 on Tuesday morning, and the funeral Mass is immediately following the wake."

"It seems like people are shortening services these days," Sam said. "I remember when the wake and funeral was a three-day affair."

"That's true. But it means that Kate might be free tomorrow. I have her phone number, so I'll text her to see if she could meet with us."

Connie shot off a quick text, and a few minutes later, Kate replied that she was indeed free the following morning and that she would meet Connie and Sam at *Just Jewelry* at 11:00.

Chapter 7

ON MONDAY MORNING, the sound of a text message woke Connie up just before her alarm was due to go off.

It was Elyse.

I'm just about to leave for Palm Paradise to pick up some things for Aunt Gertrude. They are releasing her from the hospital today, and she asked for a change of clothes.

Let me know when you get here, Connie replied. *I'll come with you for moral support while you get her clothes.*

Connie hopped in the shower and got ready for work. Just as she finished drying her hair, Elyse texted her back.

Just got here. Can you meet me at Gertrude's?

Within five minutes, Elyse was unlocking the door to Gertrude's fifth-floor condo with the key that Gertrude hid under her welcome mat.

"Thanks for coming," Elyse said. "Just give me five minutes to pack some clean clothes."

"I'll go into the kitchen and make sure there's food in the fridge," Connie said.

"Good idea."

Connie entered Gertrude's kitchen and had to laugh when she saw her apron hanging on the wall, which said "Never trust a skinny cook." Connie decided to tidy up so Gertrude wouldn't be greeted with a messy kitchen when she returned home.

She got a trash bag from beneath the sink and threw away an empty bag of barbecue potato chips. Then she opened a paper bag for recycling and rinsed out an empty container of extra spicy salsa.

Connie looked inside the refrigerator to make sure there was plenty of food and was happy to see that it was well stocked. There was a half empty takeout container, which contained two tacos and next to it, a bottle of hot sauce. Then she opened a Tupperware container filled with what appeared to be pulled pork loaded with barbecue sauce, and another with a label that read "five-alarm chili."

While she was standing in front of the open refrigerator, Elyse called from behind. "I've got what I need. How does the food situation look? Should I make a grocery store run?"

"Come here, Elyse. You've got to see this."

Connie showed her the empty bag of barbecue chips and container of spicy salsa. Then she stepped to the side, revealing the contents of the fridge.

Elyse examined each item, one by one. "I never realized how much spicy food Aunt Gertrude eats! My goodness, if I ate like this, I'd be popping antacids after every meal."

Connie laughed loudly, mostly from relief. "You and me both. I guess we know what caused the burning in her chest."

Elyse snapped a few photos with her phone. "I'm texting these to my mother so she can show Aunt Gertrude's doctor. I don't know if I'm ecstatic that she's okay or furious that she put us through this."

"Go easy on her, Elyse. Remember how scared you were that you might lose her."

Elyse sighed. "I know. I will."

By the time Connie returned to her condo, Sam was having breakfast.

"I thought you were still sleeping," he said. "I was wondering if I should wake you up."

Connie relayed what they found in Gertrude's kitchen, and Sam got a good chuckle out of it. "I'm glad to hear that everything is okay. Elyse must be relieved."

Connie had breakfast, then took Ginger for her morning walk. She and Sam arrived at *Just Jewelry* a few minutes before 9:00. Since they weren't meeting with Kate until 11:00, Sam decided to walk the beach.

He returned at 10:30 with three coffees, and they filled Grace in on their conversation with Kelly the previous day.

Kate arrived right at 11:00, and the three decided to talk about the investigation away from the store, in case any customers came in. They found a secluded spot on the beach where nobody would overhear their conversation.

"We don't have a ton of news for you yet," Connie said to Kate, "but we wanted to talk to you in person to let you know about a few discoveries."

They told Kate about Trevor's suspicions that Jeff and Kelly were having an affair and about their conversation with Kelly the previous afternoon. Connie hated bringing up the possibility of Jeff's infidelity to Rachel, but they had to be transparent with Kate, because they needed her help.

"Wow, you guys are gutsy," Kate said. "You just showed up unannounced at this woman's house?"

"We would have left immediately if we felt we were in any danger," Connie said. "Kelly denied that there was anything inappropriate about her relationship with Jeff. She's a single mom, and judging from the condition of her home, she could be telling the truth about Jeff helping her with household repairs."

"That does sound like Jeff," Kate said. "I know I'm biased because I'm his sister, but I don't believe that Jeff would have been unfaithful to Rachel. Kelly is probably telling the truth."

"I hope you're right," Connie said. "But it still bothers me that Trevor suspected infidelity. According to Trevor, that's why he and Jeff weren't speaking. If that were true, it would explain why neither of them would tell you the reason. Jeff wouldn't have wanted to admit his infidelity to his sister, and Trevor could have been trying to spare you the pain of knowing that information."

Kate leaned back on her elbows and reflected. "I suppose it's possible, but you guys didn't know Jeff the way I did. I appreciate that you're considering every possible angle, but I just don't believe my brother was having an affair." Kate paused. "But, then again…"

"What is it?" Connie asked.

"Over the past couple of days, I've been reflecting on Jeff's behavior during the last few months of his life. The more I think about it, the more I'm realizing that Jeff wasn't himself."

"In what way?" Sam asked.

"He seemed distracted. It felt as though he wasn't truly present when you were talking to him. Rachel even commented that he hadn't been spending as much time at home lately. He said that all of his activities were work-related, but I really hope that it wasn't because he was having an affair."

"It's possible that he wasn't," Sam said. "I know from experience that growing a business, especially a non-profit, can take a toll on a marriage. It can be all-consuming. That could easily have been the reason why Jeff wasn't home as often."

"Sam's right." At least Connie hoped he was. "Unfortunately, we still don't have a lot to go on. I wish we could be more help, but with so little information, this doesn't look promising."

"I hope the police are having more success than we are," Kate said.

"It's funny you should mention that. Sam and I had dinner with Zach last night. He confirmed that Jeff didn't receive a text from any of the children or teens in his after-school program. In fact, they all have confirmed alibis."

"Rachel told me the same thing," Kate said. "That doesn't make sense. Why would Jeff have lied?"

"Whatever the reason, it ultimately led to his death," Connie said.

"After the two of you left Rachel's on Sunday, she was reliving her final moments with Jeff," Kate said. "Rachel said that he had been fidgety all night. He kept getting up, going to the fridge, and returning to the couch. She didn't think anything of it at the time, but in light of what happened to him, she thought it could be important. She said that Jeff kept checking his phone, as if he were expecting a text."

"Maybe he was checking the time," Connie said.

"Could be. It was a little before 8:00 when he left. Rachel said he stood abruptly and told her he had to go. He said that one of the teens needed him. But obviously he was lying. I just wish we knew why."

"I don't know, but the key to finding out what happened to Jeff lies in the answer to that question," Connie said. "How can we figure out why Jeff left his house?"

Kate thought for a moment. "The wake and funeral are tomorrow. Afterward, many of our family and friends are going to *McGinty's Restaurant* for the funeral reception. I could ask around a little bit and keep my ears open. A lot of Jeff's friends will be there, so I'll see if anyone noticed anything suspicious."

"Are you sure you want to do that?" Sam asked. "You should mourn your brother's death in peace, without a task like that on your shoulders."

Kate sighed. "It's not ideal, but I might not have another chance to see so many of Jeff's friends all at once. I think I need to take advantage of this opportunity. Besides, the best way for me to have any semblance of peace over my brother's death is to find out what happened." Kate paused. "But wait, what if the two of you came to the luncheon? I can introduce you to some of Jeff's friends - the ones who knew him best. That way, if I have trouble breaking away from family and friends, you guys could be my backup."

"Won't our attendance look odd?" Connie asked. "We barely knew Jeff."

"They won't know that. I'll just say that you and I have become close since I started carrying your Fair Trade product, and I asked you to come for moral support."

"If you're sure we wouldn't be intruding," Connie said, looking at Sam for his approval.

Sam nodded.

"Normally, I'm alone in the shop on Tuesdays, but since Sam is in town, Grace and Abby are both planning to work so I can have some time off. It won't be a problem if I'm gone for a couple of hours."

"Perfect. Thanks, you two. This means a lot to me. I'll text you the address of the restaurant. We will be arriving after the graveside service, so we should be there by 1:00."

"Then I guess we'll see you tomorrow at 1:00," Sam said.

Chapter 8

CONNIE SPENT THE REST of Monday in the shop while Sam took Ginger and left to enjoy a leisurely day.

He returned at 9:00 that evening to pick her up.

"You look nice and relaxed," Connie said when he came through the door. His skin had a sun-kissed tone, and the tension seemed to be melting from his shoulders.

"Ginger and I had a great day. We took a long walk along Sapphire Beach Boulevard, then I brought her upstairs and went for a swim in the gulf. I also called both of my boys, and had a good chat with each of them. Then I talked to Janet for nearly an hour. She reminded me that it had been ages since we've just sat and talked for an hour. It feels nice to have time to do the little things, which aren't really so little. I don't think I realized how busy I've been until I stepped off the treadmill."

"How are your sons?" Connie asked.

"They're wonderful. Daniel is busy preparing for his wedding this spring, and Patrick will be graduating medical school a couple of weeks before Daniel's wedding. But despite his busy schedule, Patrick is doing his best not to shirk his best man duties." Sam's eyes shone with pride.

When they returned to Connie's condo, she was greeted by the smell of a home-cooked meal. "It smells fabulous in here."

"I made some chicken thighs, baked potatoes, and peas and carrots. I left everything out in case you haven't eaten yet. I wasn't sure if you usually have dinner at work or wait until you get home."

Connie dashed into the kitchen and admired the feast. "I had a late lunch and only a granola bar for dinner, so I can't wait to dig in. Sometimes I'm too tired to cook, so dinner only consists of cereal. This would have been one of those nights."

"I took Ginger for a walk just before I picked you up, so she is all set for the night."

Connie glanced at her spaniel, half asleep in front of the sliding glass doors in the living room.

"Wow, I guess there's nothing to do but relax and enjoy dinner. Thanks, Sam."

She heated up a plate of food and ate it on a TV tray in the living room while they watched a movie. They both decided to call it an early night so they would be well rested for the funeral reception the following day.

On Tuesday morning, Connie put on a black floral-print dress and a carnelian cabochon necklace with a matching bracelet and earrings, which she had recently made and decided to keep for herself, rather than sell them. She got a ride into work with Grace so that Sam could stay at home and relax until the funeral reception.

Sam picked Connie up at *Just Jewelry* at 12:45 as planned, and they drove to the end of the boulevard where *McGinty's Restaurant* was located. The hostess accompanied them to a function room overlooking the Gulf of Mexico. The large room was filled with people, somberly milling about.

As Connie and Sam perused the room, Kate spotted them and gave them a curt wave. She excused herself from the couple she was speaking with and made her way over to Connie and Sam. Connie gave her a big hug. "I'm so sorry, Kate. I can't imagine how hard this day must be for you."

Kate gave her a half smile and nodded. "It's a tough one. Jeff's death was so unexpected. I think I'm still in shock." She glanced around the room. "So is everyone else for that matter. It feels like I'm having a bad dream."

"Maybe it wasn't such a good idea for us to come," Connie said. "We should let you mourn in peace. Why don't we deal with the investigation another time?"

"Don't be foolish," Kate said. "I am so grateful to the two of you for taking time out of your day to be here. Why don't you get some food and then I'll introduce you to some friends of Jeff's?"

Connie and Sam lined up at the long buffet. The server put a slice of pot roast, red potatoes, and carrots on each of their plates while Kate greeted the attendees. When they were finished, she escorted Connie and Sam to one of the large round tables scattered throughout the room.

"You guys met Trevor." Kate gestured toward a woman sitting next to him. "This is Justine, his wife."

Kate motioned toward another couple at the table. The man wore a black silk suit, and the woman was in a black designer dress. "This is Bill, a longtime friend of Jeff's, and his wife Audrey."

And to a third couple, she said, "And meet Tim and Lucy. Tim worked with Jeff in the after-school program."

Kate pulled over two empty chairs from the table next to them, and the others pulled their chairs closer to make room for them. Kate gestured for Connie and Sam to sit down.

"It's nice to meet you all. My name is Connie, and this is my friend, Sam."

"Connie is a dear friend," Kate said. "She owns a jewelry shop downtown, and we carry some of her Fair Trade product."

Connie realized that she didn't know very much about Kate's personal life and she hoped she wouldn't be put to the test, since Kate had made it sound as if they were close friends.

As Kate was leaving, Bill stood up. "I was just going to the bar. Can I get anyone a drink?"

Audrey made eye contact with her husband. "Isn't it a little early, honey?"

He looked around the table at the others, then back at Audrey. "I guess you're right. It's been such a long day that it feels like it should be dinner time."

Audrey smiled and Connie thought she saw Tim and Lucy breathe a sigh of relief.

"So," Trevor said to Connie, sarcastically "I didn't realize you and Kate were such good friends. I've never heard Kate mention you until Saturday."

Connie let the remark slide with a polite smile.

"Tim, have you been working with Jeff in the after-school program since its inception a couple of years ago?" Sam asked.

Tim raised his eyebrows at Sam. "I didn't realize you were so familiar with the program."

"Jeff and I had dinner together the night he died. I founded a non-profit in the Boston area thirteen years ago, so he wanted to pick my brain. He was a very driven young man with big dreams for his non-profit. It's such a tragedy that he was taken so young."

"That means you were one of the last people to see Jeff alive," Tim said.

"Yes. I was with him just a few hours before his death."

Tim let out a sigh. "I've been involved with the program from the beginning. I'm a high school teacher, but I have worked part-time for Jeff since he opened the doors. Bill here was on the board of directors until a short time ago."

"Jeff, Trevor, and I go way back," Bill said. "We were best friends in college. Jeff and Trevor studied Social Work, and I double majored in Business and Fine Arts. I was on the board to offer my business expertise. I used to tell Jeff that I had been involved in a few non-profits over the years, even though all of my businesses were meant to *make* a profit."

Bill chuckled and Audrey rolled her eyes. "Billy never gets tired of that joke."

"So, you're no longer on the board?" Sam asked.

"No. My career got too demanding, and I had to leave a few months ago. I agreed to remain a sounding board for Jeff, but I could no longer commit to the level of time it required to be a board member. I was head of the fundraising committee, so it ate up a good chunk of my limited spare time."

"That's understandable," Connie said. "You mentioned that Jeff studied Social Work. What did he do before he started the program?" Connie knew the answer to that question, but she wanted to get them talking.

"He worked as a case manager for Child Welfare for seven years, but he saw a need for a consistent presence in the kids' lives, so he founded the after-school program," Tim said. "The program was his baby. He was planning to expand and offer additional services to the community, as well, but, unfortunately, he never got the chance."

"What type of business are you involved in?" Sam asked Bill.

"I'm an art dealer. I'm the middleman between artists and people looking to acquire art."

"You mean collectors?" Sam asked.

"Exactly. Collectors, galleries, museums. My job requires traveling, so I've had to cut out a lot of non-work commitments."

"That's fascinating," Sam said. "What an interesting line of work."

"I love it. After spending a year in Paris during college, I decided to double major."

"Paris is such an incredible city," Sam said. "My wife and I spent a month backpacking across Europe right after we were married. We, too, developed a passion for art history. Many of our friends are collectors."

Bill took his wallet from his suit blazer pocket, pulled out a business card, and wrote something on it. Then he handed the card to Sam. "Here is my information, in case you or your friends are looking to acquire any new pieces. You'll find my prices are unbeatable."

"Bill is right," Audrey said. "You won't find better prices in all of Florida."

"I wrote down some information on an exhibition at a gallery next week for a local artist, Thomas Carmichael," Bill continued. "If you're still in town, please come by and I will introduce you to the artist."

"Please do come," Audrey said. "We'd love to see you there."

"Thank you. I just might take you up on that," Sam said, slipping the card into his pocket.

Trevor was quietly observing the exchange, and so was Connie. She had almost forgotten how well Sam could work a room. Or a table in this case.

"I can't imagine what you all must be going through, losing one of your best friends so tragically," Sam continued. "Since the three of you knew Jeff well, I have to ask. Do you have any idea who might have killed him? Did he have any enemies that you know about?"

Trevor ran a hand through his hair, and Bill's shoulders grew stiff. Why did they both seem so tense?

"I already shared my thoughts with you," Trevor said.

Bill pushed away a full plate of food. "I wish I knew. All I know is that Audrey and I were together the night Jeff was killed. If you'll excuse me, there are some people I'd like to see."

"Of course," Sam said.

"Please excuse Bill," Audrey said. "It's a difficult time."

"I can imagine," Sam said. "We didn't mean to upset him. But the sooner Jeff's killer is discovered, the sooner his family can grieve and move on with their lives."

Audrey smiled, then joined her husband, who had made his way to the other side of the room.

Tim cleared his throat. "I don't know what happened to Jeff," he said, "but he was definitely distracted over the past few months. When I asked him about it, he just said that he felt a lot of pressure to make the after-school program work. He was the type of guy who took everyone's problems upon himself. Trevor and I were always telling him that he couldn't save the whole world, but he had a hard time accepting that."

"Are you sure you didn't notice anything else unusual?" Connie asked. "You seem to have spent a lot of time with him."

Tim furrowed his brow. "There *was* one thing, but it's probably nothing."

"What is it?" Connie and Sam asked in unison.

"I was downtown last week, and I saw Jeff in a heated argument with a man named Stewart. I recognized him, because he would sometimes pick up his son, Andy, from the after-school program. Usually, Kelly, the boy's mother, would pick him up, but occasionally Stewart would come. Anyway, he was really laying into Jeff. I asked Jeff about it later and he said not to worry about it. He said that Stewart was just going through a rough patch and needed someone to take it out on. But Stewart looked pretty angry to me."

Chapter 9

BY THE TIME Connie, Sam, and the others at their table finished eating, the reception hall was beginning to clear out, so Connie and Sam returned to *Just Jewelry*.

Tuesdays were one of the store's slower days, but Connie wanted to stick around, anyway, to help Grace until Abby's shift began.

When Abby arrived at 4:00, Connie and Sam caught Grace and Abby up on the investigation. Sam became animated as he took the lead in relaying what they had learned from their conversations and observations at the reception.

Sam was proving to be a worthy sidekick. He had never been the type to sit around and do nothing, even on vacation, and now that he was getting some of his energy back, Connie was happy to put it to good use. The case seemed to animate him, and he seemed more like himself than he had since he arrived on Friday.

"So, who are your suspects so far?" Abby asked.

"There's definitely something strange going on with Trevor," Connie said. "He wasn't happy that we showed up asking questions at the reception."

"It sounds like Jeff and Trevor had been good friends. Did something happen between them that would give Trevor a motive to kill Jeff?"

"We're not sure," Connie said. "According to Kate, they had some type of falling out a few months ago. She doesn't know what happened. Neither Jeff or Trevor wanted to talk about it with her or Rachel."

"Trevor mentioned to us that he thought Jeff might have been having an affair with a woman named Kelly, since he was visiting her house many afternoons during his lunch break," Sam added. "We talked with Kelly, but she insisted Jeff was only helping her with repairs around the house. She is a recently separated single mom, and she was having some financial troubles. She maintained that the whole thing was innocent."

"Did you believe her?" Grace asked.

"I'm not sure. She obviously wouldn't admit to having an affair, but Trevor knew Jeff well, and he suspected they might be," Connie said.

"But Kate told us that it wasn't uncommon for Jeff to help people in need, especially the families of the kids in his after-school program. So, it's possible that Kelly was telling the truth," Sam added.

"If Jeff and Kelly *were* having an affair, that could have provided a motive for either Kelly or Rachel to kill him," Grace said.

"That's true. And neither of them has an alibi for the time Jeff was murdered," Connie said.

"Were you able to see Rachel and Kelly interact at the funeral reception?"

"Kelly wasn't there," Sam said. "According to Kate, she was at the wake that morning, but she couldn't stay for the funeral, because she had to get to work."

Grace rubbed her chin. "That doesn't seem like a lot to go on. It sounds like you need more information."

"I agree. I wish we could talk to Kelly's husband, Stewart," Connie said. "Tim, who worked with Jeff at the after-school program, saw Stewart and Jeff in a heated argument. It might not be a coincidence that Jeff was killed shortly after arguing with Stewart."

"If Jeff and Kelly were having an affair and Stewart found out about it, that could be a strong motive, as well," Sam said. "Especially since he and Kelly are not yet divorced."

"Even if they *weren't* having an affair, if Kelly's husband *thought* they were, that could also be a motive," Abby said.

Connie let out a sigh. "The problem is, we don't really have any way of talking to Stewart."

"Maybe Kate will have an idea," Sam suggested.

"She might. But I think we should give Kate some space. After all, she just buried her brother. Why don't we wait and reach out to her tomorrow?" Connie suggested. "Maybe we'll have a fresh perspective if we let it go for a while."

"It's been a slow day," Grace said. "You two should take off and do something fun."

Abby agreed. "I can handle the store for the rest of the day. There aren't a lot of people out and about downtown."

"That's not a bad idea," Connie said. "I want to make sure Sam enjoys plenty of time outdoors breathing in the fresh air before I send him back to Massachusetts."

Sam pretended to shiver. "Now that I've been spoiled with seventy and eighty degree weather, I'm not looking forward to facing the cold winter again."

"We still have some time before the sun sets. Let's drop Ginger off at home and enjoy the sunset from the beach."

"I think Stephanie mentioned that she would be finishing work early today," Grace said. "She had some compensation time coming and decided to take the afternoon off. I'll bet she'd love to join you."

"That sounds great. I'll text Elyse, as well. It will be a great opportunity for Sam to meet my two Florida besties."

Connie sent her friends a group text, and within an hour, Connie, Sam, Elyse, and Stephanie were relaxing on the beach and chatting.

"Next time you come to the beach," Elyse said to Sam, "you should have Connie bring her paddleboard."

"I prefer something a little faster." Sam pointed to two jet skis skimming across the gulf. "Those are more my speed. I think I might rent one while Connie's at work one afternoon."

"You won't regret it," Stephanie said. "They're a ton of fun."

"I feel like we're old friends, Sam," Elyse said. "We've heard so much about you. I hope you're not too mad at us for encouraging Connie to move here and open her jewelry shop. But I'd be lying if I said I was sorry."

Sam smiled. "Oh, that's right, *you're* the one who planted the idea in Connie's mind. Well, seeing how happy she is, I guess I can find it in my heart to forgive you."

"Speaking of Connie being happy," Elyse said with a mischievous smile, "have you met Zach?"

Sam smiled at Connie. "Yes, I've had the pleasure. He and Connie picked me up at the airport, and we also had dinner together on Sunday night. Speaking as someone who has known Connie for thirteen years, I think they make a sweet couple."

"We wholeheartedly agree," Stephanie said with a broad smile.

Elyse smiled playfully. "I thought there might have been a ring on Christmas."

Connie turned toward Sam. "She's unrelenting!"

"Well, there's always Valentine's Day," Elyse said. "It's just over a month away."

"I also met your beau, Gallagher McKeon," Sam said to Stephanie. "I had dinner at his restaurant on Saturday evening with Jeff Collins. Gallagher's a great guy."

Connie shot Sam a grateful smile for changing the subject, and he replied with a discreet wink.

"Oh, yes, that's right," Elyse said. "Josh mentioned that you were one of the last people to see Jeff alive. What a tragedy. He was so young and such a solid member of the community."

"I didn't realize you knew Jeff," Connie said.

"I didn't know him well, but I followed what he was doing with the after-school program. It was a great contribution to the town. He encountered some naysayers in the beginning. Many people thought that Sapphire Beach didn't need an after-school program, since it's a middle class community, but there are a number of working moms who really appreciate that it exists."

Stephanie chuckled. "If I know Connie, she has the two of you conducting an investigation of your own, especially since you were with Jeff the night he died."

"It's providing me with a worthwhile puzzle to solve while I'm on vacation," Sam said. He winked at Stephanie. "Don't tell my wife, though. She thinks that I'm spending all my time at the beach."

While they were talking, the setting sun set the sky ablaze. It turned it a fiery orange as the sun slowly descended behind the horizon, leaving Sam in awe.

"That never gets old," Connie said.

Sam snapped a plethora of photos, including a selfie of Connie and himself, which he texted to Janet.

Sam read aloud his wife's reply. "Glad Connie has you relaxing."

The women laughed.

"I guess you're right," Elyse said. "You probably shouldn't mention the investigation."

"I think I'll wait until I get home to tell her about it. What she doesn't know won't hurt her."

"By the way, how is Gertrude?" Connie asked. "She's been on my mind since we found all that spicy food in her house yesterday morning."

Elyse shook her head. "She seems to be fine. The doctor said that her diet definitely could have mimicked a heart attack. I paid her a visit this morning, and she seems to be okay. She's bummed that the doctor has her on a bland diet, although I'm not convinced that she's going to stick to it. But at least in the future we'll be aware of the situation."

"I'm so relieved to hear that. I'll be sure to drop by to try to cheer her up," Connie said.

For the next few minutes until the sun had completely set, Sam and Connie caught Elyse and Stephanie up on their investigation so far.

"I know Kelly Robinson and her husband, Stewart," Elyse said. "I was so sorry to hear that they separated. Stewart called me to help him find a rental. I don't specialize in rentals, but I felt so badly that I made an exception."

"Could you tell if he was hoping to reconcile with Kelly?" Connie asked. If he was, and he believed Kelly was involved with Jeff, that could have been a motive to kill him.

"He definitely was," Elyse said. "He seemed really depressed about the separation, and he insisted that I find a rental without a lease, which was no easy task. He didn't want to commit to a lease, because he was hoping to move back in with his wife and son. He also didn't want to be too far from them. It was nearly impossible to find something that met his specifications, but I finally managed to find him a small two-bedroom house the next street over."

"Stewart's on our list of people to talk to," Connie said. "But I know it would be a breach of confidence to give us his address, so I won't ask."

"Thank you. And it's not like you can knock on his door and say, 'Hi, we're wondering if the wife you would like to reconcile with was involved with another man, and if so, did you kill him?'"

Connie laughed at Elyse's dramatic choice of words. "Maybe not. But we have to figure out a way to talk to him."

Elyse reflected for a moment. "Well, I happen to know that he took a second job to make ends meet after he and his wife separated. He's a landscaper by day, and he also works at *Gulf Coast Sporting Goods* on Sundays and Thursdays. I saw him last week when I was there with Emma looking at beach volleyball equipment."

"I know that store," Connie said. "Emma mentioned that her kneepads are wearing thin, so I've been meaning to stop by to pick her up a new pair to thank her for helping me out in the store from time to time. Sam and I could take a ride by on Thursday morning and ask Stewart a few questions."

"That's a perfect excuse. And the kneepads are totally unnecessary, but Emma is going to love you for that," Elyse said.

Chapter 10

WEDNESDAY WAS UNEVENTFUL. Sam spent the day relaxing at the Palm Paradise pool while Connie worked at *Just Jewelry*. Even though Grace and Abby were willing to take on additional shifts while Sam was visiting, she didn't want to overwork them. So, she worked from opening until closing and insisted that Grace leave early.

On Thursday morning, Connie and Sam opened *Just Jewelry* with Grace, then went straight to *Gulf Coast Sporting Goods* in hopes of talking to Stewart. Fortunately, there were only a few other customers in the store, and they were on the other side of the building.

A sales associate greeted them warmly as they entered the store. "Can I help you find something today?"

Connie glanced at the man's name tag, which read "Stewart."

Perfect.

"Yes, thank you. Could you help me find some beach volleyball kneepads for a thirteen-year-old?" Connie asked.

"Absolutely," Stewart said. He walked them over to a section that contained rows of volleyballs, nets, shoes, and other equipment. He pulled a pair of kneepads from the shelf. "These are great for the beach. They're our top seller."

They were similar to the ones Connie had seen when she was exploring online the other day. "Perfect. I'll take them."

Stewart started to bring them to the front of the store, but Connie slowed her gait.

"Is there something else I can help you with?" he asked.

"Actually, there was one more thing. We were hoping you could answer a few questions about Jeff Collins."

Stewart stopped abruptly. "Who are you again?"

"We are friends of Jeff's sister, Kate. My name is Connie, and this is my friend, Sam."

Sam nodded. "I was with Jeff shortly before he passed away. Kate asked us to help her discover the truth about what happened to her brother."

"What happened to Jeff was tragic, but I'm afraid I barely knew the man. I don't know anything that could help you."

Connie opted for the direct approach. "Why were you arguing with Jeff downtown shortly before his death?"

Stewart's jaw dropped.

"A friend of Jeff's saw the two of you in a heated discussion. What were you arguing about?" Connie asked.

Stewart glanced around the store, but nobody was within earshot. "That's a personal matter."

Connie persisted. "Personal enough to be a motive for murder?"

Stewart shook his head and let out a sharp breath. "Of course not. I never touched the guy. I merely asked him what his car was doing in front of my wife's house several afternoons a week. Not that it's any of your business, but my wife and I are temporarily separated, and I live on the next street over. I stayed home from work with a cold one day a few weeks ago and I was feeling better by the afternoon, so I went by to drop off my son's favorite book, which he forgot at my house the previous weekend. There was a strange car in the driveway, so I parked across the street and waited to see who it was. I immediately recognized Jeff from the after-school program. I started driving by the house during my lunch break to see if this was a regular occurrence, and, sure enough, it was."

"According to Kelly, Jeff was helping her with some odd jobs around the house," Sam said.

"That's what he told me, too. At first, I believed him. But then I discovered that Jeff's help went beyond household repairs."

"What do you mean?" Connie asked.

"Jeff paid Kelly's rent last month. Kelly recently lost one of her jobs - we both work two jobs to make ends meet now that we're supporting two households," Stewart explained. "I try to help Kelly as best I can, but I can't afford to pay her rent. I took it upon myself to ask Joe, Kelly's landlord, for more time. I didn't want my son to have to move on top of all he's been going through with our separation. That's when Joe informed me that Jeff had paid the rent for her."

"So, that's why you were arguing with Jeff?" Sam asked.

Stewart crossed his arms and nodded. "I didn't set out to argue with him. I was downtown running errands and I saw him talking with a friend. They looked like they were having an intense conversation."

"Can you describe the friend?" Connie asked.

"He was average height, stocky build, light brown hair. I don't remember much more. I was more focused on Jeff."

"That sounds like Trevor," Sam said.

Connie pulled out her phone and did a social media search for Trevor Hines. She showed his photo to Stewart. "Was this the guy?"

"Yup, that's him."

"It's Trevor," Connie said.

That meant Jeff and Trevor were together a few days before Jeff's death. Why did Trevor say he hadn't seen Jeff in months?

"Anyway, they were having coffee at an outdoor café," Stewart said. "I didn't want to interrupt, so I hung low and waited until they were finished. When Trevor left, I approached Jeff and asked him if he was having an affair with my wife. He denied it and said he was only helping her with some things around the house. I asked about the rent money, and he said he sometimes used donations from the after-school program to help the families of the kids he served."

"Did you believe him?"

"I didn't know what to believe. What it comes down to is that he was either helping my wife and son or taking advantage of them. Kelly denied any wrongdoing, and she's not the type to have an affair. Jeff *is* married, after all. But she was also vulnerable, and Jeff came in like some savior with his after-school program and the rent money." Stewart clenched his fists. "I don't trust the guy, but I didn't kill him."

"I'm sure it would be hard to watch your soon-to-be-ex-wife date someone else," Connie said.

Stewart's eyes grew somber. "For the record, we're not getting divorced if I can help it. Kelly and I just need a little time apart. I am trying to give her some space so we can figure things out. There's nothing I want more than for Kelly, Andy, and me to be a family again."

Stewart seemed sincere. It was obvious that he truly did want to reconcile with his wife. But would he have killed Jeff if he thought Jeff had been an obstacle to his plans?

Connie and Sam thanked Stewart for his time. Then Connie paid for Emma's thank-you gift and they left.

On their way back downtown, Connie and Sam made an impromptu stop at a coffee shop to pick up some treats to take back to *Just Jewelry.* It was a good thing they did. When they returned, Grace was sitting with Kelly Robinson at the long oak table in Connie's shop, which she used primarily to make jewelry and to teach, but it also did double duty as a gathering spot. Grace had her hand on Kelly's, who looked as if she had lost her best friend.

"Kelly," Connie said, "Sam and I were just talking about you." She wasn't sure if she should mention where they had come from. But it turned out she already knew.

"Grace told me you were talking with Stewart," Kelly said.

Connie and Sam sat at the table, and Sam opened their box of treats. "We just got these freshly baked cookies. Please help yourselves."

Kelly took a chocolate chip cookie, and Grace opted for a peanut butter cookie.

"That's true," Connie said. "We went to the funeral reception after Jeff's services on Tuesday, and someone told us that Jeff and Stewart were seen in a heated discussion a few days before Jeff died."

"That doesn't surprise me," Kelly said. "Stewart was convinced that there was something going on between Jeff and me, because he saw Jeff's car parked in my driveway. I'd never seen him so angry. He even somehow discovered that Jeff's organization paid my rent last month."

"Is Stewart the jealous type?" Sam asked.

"He can be. And I know he saw Jeff as a threat, even though that couldn't be further from the truth. Jeff was only a friend. Stewart was the one who was unfaithful. At least I thought he was. I don't know anything anymore."

Tears streamed down Kelly's face. "I really hope Stewart didn't do it."

Grace moved her chair closer to Kelly and put her arm around her shoulders. Kelly leaned her head against Grace.

"I'm so sorry," Kelly said. "I didn't come over to fall apart. I came to ask you if you had made any progress in your investigation, and I met this kind woman. The next thing I knew, I was pouring out my life story."

Connie smiled. She could easily understand how that could happen. Grace's maternal demeanor made it easy to open up to her.

"Honey, don't worry. You must feel as though you're carrying the weight of the world on your shoulders. You're a single mom, you just lost one of your jobs, and a trusted friend was murdered over the weekend. You don't have anything to apologize for."

Connie observed Kelly as Grace stroked her long red hair. She looked like she was struggling to get through the day, not like someone capable of planning and executing a murder.

"I can't even look for another job, because the after-school program is closed until they can figure out what to do in Jeff's absence," Kelly said. "It could take months for the board of directors to hire a new executive director. I really hope Stewart didn't do anything stupid. He hasn't been himself since we separated. How would I explain to my eight-year-old that his father killed his mentor? And how would we make ends meet without his child support if Stewart went to jail?"

Grace patted Kelly's shoulder. "Don't think like that. You could be wasting your energy worrying about something that will never happen."

Kelly inhaled deeply and wiped her tears with a tissue that Grace had given her. "You're right. I have to pull myself together for Andy's sake. I need to be strong for him."

"You'll get through this," Grace said. "And don't be a stranger. Take Andy in for a visit some time. I'd love to meet your little boy."

Kelly smiled and nodded. Then she wrote something on a piece of paper and handed it to Connie. "Here's my phone number. Please call me if you learn anything or if you have any other questions about Jeff. Now, more than ever, I need to know who killed him so I can be sure that Stewart wasn't involved."

Connie punched Kelly's number into her phone and saved it in her address book. "Got it. I'll let you know if we learn anything. And here," Connie said, resealing the box of cookies and handing it to Kelly. "Bring these home for Andy."

"Thank you. I'd better get back to work."

Grace walked Kelly to the door and gave her a hug before she left. "I don't think that poor child is guilty of murder," she said when she rejoined Connie and Sam. "She's just trying to get through life one day at a time, and Jeff was more help to her alive. She wouldn't have killed him."

"I tend to agree," Connie said. "And I really hope Stewart is innocent. I wouldn't want to see Kelly and her son suffer another devastating blow."

Chapter 11

SAM STOOD AND WALKED over to one of the front windows overlooking the street. Then, he turned around abruptly and made a bee line for Connie, who was still seated at the table. "I just got an idea. Could I borrow your car?"

"Of course," Connie said. "But where are you going?"

"First let me see if it will work out. Then I will tell you my plan."

Connie tossed Sam the car key. "Not even a hint?"

He winked and was out the door within seconds.

Connie looked at Grace, then shook her head and laughed. "That's Sam for you. Always up to something mysterious. It's good to see he's getting back to his old self."

Connie and Grace attended to the afternoon customers, and before Connie knew it, Grace's shift was over. A couple of hours later, Abby arrived.

"I wonder where Sam went," Grace said before she left. "I thought he would have been back from his secret errand by now."

"Oh, I wouldn't worry about Sam. He has a good time wherever he goes. He's probably captivating some new friends with stories of one of his many adventures."

About an hour later, he returned.

"Well, hello there," Connie said. "I was beginning to think you decided to go back to Massachusetts."

"Not a chance," Sam said with a chuckle.

"Are you going to keep me waiting any longer or tell me where you went?"

He pulled a chair away from the table and sat on it backwards so he could face Connie. "I just got back from the offices of the after-school program hoping to catch Tim. I forgot that he was a teacher, so I got an ice cream and went back at 3:00. Luckily, Tim was there working on some paperwork.

Remember how Kelly told us that the program would be closed until they found a replacement for Jeff?"

Connie nodded.

"Well, I know that Jeff would be devastated that the program had to shut its doors, even temporarily. I told Tim that since I was going to be in town for another ten days, I'd be happy to help him by volunteering in the afternoons. The children and teens arrive at 2:30 and the program ends at 5:30, so it would only be a few hours per day. The volunteers help children with homework and lead games and activities, so it will be a nice change of pace. That way I'll have something to do in the afternoons while you're working in the store. Don't tell Janet, though. I promised her I'd take it easy during my vacation."

Connie tended to agree with Janet on that one. How would she explain it to Janet if Sam returned home more tired than when he arrived? "Are you sure you want to make that kind of commitment? Kids can be exhausting."

"I'm positive. In fact, I know I'll enjoy just being a volunteer and not the person in charge. I'm beginning to see that it's all the pressure of raising money and managing an ever-growing organization that has me stressed. I think these kids will help me to get back in touch with my roots. In fact, working with children is my first love as a volunteer. That's what Janet and I originally did in South America."

"That's right," Connie said to Abby. "I almost forgot how good Sam is with kids. I've seen him in action several times during our trips to visit our partner organizations."

"A few hours a day of volunteering will be a healthy diversion. I have a good feeling about it. Tim said that a few teachers at his school have offered to volunteer, as well, until they can find more permanent help, so he's taking it as a sign that he should reopen. I also offered to be Tim's sounding board while he puts together a search committee to fill Jeff's position. Tim said he thought long and hard about applying for the position himself, but he wants to remain in teaching. However, since he was the only employee of the program besides Jeff, the board of directors has asked him to head up the search committee."

"I think it proved providential that you had dinner with Jeff the night he died," Connie said. "Since he shared with you his vision for the organization, you'll be in a good position to help advise Tim."

"That's another reason I was gone for so long. Tim and I were discussing the future of the program and what qualities they should be looking for in Jeff's replacement. Tim is going to spend the rest of this week pulling together a committee and writing up a job description to present to the board at the end of next week, but while I was there, he called the chairman and a few others, and they agreed to allow him to reopen."

"That's great news, Sam," Connie said. "Your help will be invaluable. It was definitely meant to be that you met Jeff. Not only are you helping me solve his murder, but you are the perfect person to help Tim."

"I feel the same way. And to be honest, I know Janet means well, but the idea of sitting around all day just isn't me. I've rested plenty in the past five days. Now I'm ready to make myself useful."

Connie had so much admiration for Sam. He could be offering his consulting services to for-profit businesses for a hefty sum, but instead he chose to dedicate himself to a fantastic cause.

While they were talking, a few customers walked into *Just Jewelry*. They were so boisterous that Connie almost didn't notice Kate, who entered just behind them.

"Kate, we didn't expect to see you today. How are you doing?" Connie asked.

She looked a little better than she did at the funeral reception, but not much.

"I'm hanging in there. I wanted to come by yesterday to talk to you, but one thing after another kept coming up. I was on the phone most of the day with friends of Jeff, who were calling to check in. It's nice of them to express their concern, but it can be exhausting repeating the same thing over and over."

Abby sprang into action greeting the customers, so Connie and Sam could spend some time with Kate.

"I know it's tiring," Sam said. "Be gentle with yourself. It's an important part of the grieving process to talk about what happened."

"You're probably right," Kate said. "But I think what I really need is some closure regarding my brother's murder. I need to know what happened and to see his killer behind bars."

Connie brought out a pitcher of iced tea that she had brewed earlier along with some cups while Abby rang up some purchases. Kate was thrilled to hear that the after-school program would reopen its doors, and she was grateful that Sam would be advising Tim.

Connie was happy to see a smile eke its way across Kate's face.

"I can't thank you enough," she said to Sam. "That's the best news I've heard all day. But the reason I'm here is because I've been wanting to tell you something that I learned at the wake. I'm not sure if this is connected to Jeff's murder, but a few people made it a point to tell me that Jeff had paid various bills for them when they were in a bind."

"Like he did for Kelly?" Connie asked.

"Exactly. Kelly Robinson was one of those people. I mentioned it to Rachel, and she didn't know anything about it. She checked their bank statements just to be sure, and she confirmed that Jeff didn't take the money from any of their personal accounts. I also asked Tim to look over the books for the non-profit, and he said that the money didn't come from there, either, as Jeff had been telling people."

"Maybe he got private donors to make contributions," Sam suggested. "Jeff had a lot of charisma and a lot of passion for those kids. It wouldn't surprise me if he found people to help out some of these families."

"I suppose that's possible," Kate said. "Maybe he didn't want to deal with the paperwork or have to get the board's permission to spend donations as he saw fit, so instead he approached people on the side."

"When Jeff and I had dinner, he shared that one of the ways he hoped to expand the organization was by adding a food pantry so he could help families when they were down and out. Maybe providing emergency financial assistance was part of his vision, too," Sam said.

As they were talking, Abby began setting up the table for Connie's jewelry-making class, which was due to start in less than an hour. Since Connie had to get back to work, she and Sam promised that they would give some thought to what their next step would be, and they all agreed to be back in touch shortly.

Kate, for her part, promised to ask around and learn what she could about what happened between Jeff and Trevor. "Now that the funeral is behind us, I want to focus my energies on finding my brother's killer."

Chapter 12

SAM DECIDED to hang around *Just Jewelry* for the rest of the evening to observe Connie in action while she taught her jewelry-making class. He opted to chat with students and customers rather than attempt to make the sea glass bracelet that the class was creating. However, in his stead, Connie completed the bracelet she used to demonstrate for the class and gave it to Sam to bring home for Janet.

When class was over, it was nearly closing time.

Connie and Abby put away the tools and supplies and straightened up the shop while Sam took Ginger for her nightly walk.

The two women chatted while they cleaned. During the busy month of January, they spent most of their time waiting on customers, so there wasn't as much time left to catch up on their personal lives. Abby was in her first year of graduate studies in American Literature at nearby Florida Sands University. She was hoping to be a professor and author once she graduated. Her love of reading helped her through a battle with leukemia as a teenager, so she hoped to instill her passion in the next generation. Connie had no doubt she would inspire young people for generations to come.

While Connie and Sam were driving home, it occurred to Connie that she hadn't talked to Zach in several days. So, after they returned home, she texted him to see how he was doing.

I'm just getting off work, Zach said. *It's been a long week. If you're home, I can stop by.*

Sounds perfect. Sam and I were just going to watch a movie for the rest of the night, and I was just about to text Grace to see if she'd like to join us.

Since Connie hadn't seen Gertrude since she got home from the hospital on Monday, she invited her over, as well. Within fifteen minutes, Zach, Grace, and Gertrude had joined Connie and Sam for a glass of Merlot and some snacks that Connie had found in her cupboards. Unfortunately, she needed to get to the grocery store, so she only had cookies and chips. Connie apologized to Gertrude for not having any healthy options.

Gertrude waved away her apology and took a couple of cookies. "Don't tell my family because they will worry needlessly, but I've made it to eighty-eight years old in perfect health. A little indigestion isn't going to kill me. Isn't it ironic how all the young folks are trying to tell me how to live my life, as if they know more about getting old than me?"

It was impossible to argue with that logic, so nobody tried.

It turned out that they didn't end up watching much of the movie. Sam and Connie started telling more stories about the early days of *Feeding the Hungry,* and Grace shared memories of her adventures with Concetta over the years. Nothing made Connie happier than to see her friends from various periods of her life become acquainted.

Eventually, the conversation turned to the investigation.

"Have you made much progress in finding Jeff's killer?" Sam asked Zach.

"We've been chasing leads all week, but it doesn't look like we'll be making an arrest anytime soon. I did speak with Tim again this evening, though. He told me you're going to help get the after-school program up and running again."

Sam nodded. "Six days of mostly sleeping in and relaxing under the sun have been wonderful, and I've certainly decompressed, but I think I'll go stir crazy if I'm idle for a minute longer."

Zach laughed. "That's probably the same attitude that helped you grow a successful non-profit."

"You're probably right. And the idea of doing direct service with children, as opposed to managing an ever-growing organization, seems to be energizing me. It feels more like reconnecting with my first love than work."

"In that case, it sounds like the perfect vacation for you," Zach said. "And I understand what you mean. As much as I love the outdoors, I think that after a week of sun and surf, I'd be ready for some kind of project, too."

"I hope Tim and the board of directors are able to keep the after-school program alive," Sam said. "I feel fortunate to have had dinner with Jeff the night he died. He shared with me many of his dreams for the program, which he hadn't yet discussed with his board of directors. One of the things he asked me to advise him on was how to best present his ideas for expanding the program to the board. I'm glad he did, because I was able to pass some of his hopes along to Tim. When we met earlier today, we also did some brainstorming on what the job description should look like as they move forward with hiring a new executive director. Tim's going to talk to Rachel to see if he's missing anything, but he is eager to begin the search."

"It's fortunate for the organization that you were here," Grace said.

Connie nodded her agreement.

"That's wonderful news," Gertrude said. She had been following the case in the newspapers. "When will they reopen?"

"Monday," Sam replied. "That will give Tim enough time to get things in order and to do the necessary criminal background check on me before I can work with the children. The other volunteers are teachers, so they automatically have one done every year."

"Tim has a solid alibi for Jeff's murder, as well as no apparent motive, so I feel comfortable with him at the helm for the time being," Zach said.

It hadn't occurred to Connie that if Jeff's murder were connected with someone involved in the after-school program, that could put the children in danger. She was glad to hear Zach was comfortable with Tim taking charge, even though he hadn't been one of Connie's suspects.

"Speaking of the success of the after-school program," Sam said, "I really hope Jeff and Kelly weren't having an affair. It would be a shame for the program's reputation to be tarnished in that way."

"Ah, so you heard about that," Zach said.

Sam looked guiltily at Connie.

"Don't worry," Zach said. "You didn't reveal anything I don't already know. I always assume Connie has her nose in my murder investigations, especially when she knows the players involved. Since she's friends with Jeff's sister and since you had dinner with the victim, I figured she'd be asking around. I'm sure you've heard about Connie's habit of solving murders in Sapphire Beach."

"Connie's parents told me about some of her adventures, especially when they were in town two Christmases ago," Sam said.

"Try to keep her out of trouble if you can," Zach said.

"I'll do my best, but you must know that's no easy task."

"Hey, you two don't have to talk about me as if I'm not in the room," Connie said.

Zach winked at Connie. "You don't listen to me when I speak to you directly, so I'll try any approach at my disposal to keep you safe."

Sam raised his hands playfully. "I'm staying out of this one."

"Don't worry, we've had this conversation many times before. I know better than to try to change Connie, so we have an agreement that I look the other way about her involvement, and she tells me the moment she feels she might be in danger. It seems to work."

"Smart man," Sam said.

Zach emptied his glass of Merlot. "I'd better get going. Tomorrow is shaping up to be a long day."

"I'm getting a little tired myself," Gertrude said. "I think I'll go back downstairs to my own condo."

Connie walked Zach and Gertrude to the door. She felt better seeing that Gertrude was back to her old self.

When Connie returned to the living room, Sam and Grace had poured the three of them another glass of wine.

"I didn't want to say anything in front of Zach, because I know that Connie likes to minimize the extent of her sleuthing when he's around," Grace said. "But I've been thinking about the case since we talked earlier today."

Connie had to struggle not to laugh with wine in her mouth. "You know me well."

"I just can't believe that Kelly could have had anything to do with Jeff's death. She is such a sweet woman, and I think she is too preoccupied with supporting her son to be involved in something so sinister. I think Trevor, Stewart, and Rachel should be your strongest suspects at this point."

Grace was a good judge of character, so Connie took her instincts on Kelly seriously.

"I hope you're right. But Trevor knew Jeff well, and he did say that he suspected they were having an affair," Sam said.

"It's always possible that Trevor was mistaken, and that Jeff's and Kelly's relationship truly was innocent," Grace said.

"Or that Trevor lied to throw us off," Connie suggested. "He did tell us that he hadn't talked to Jeff for several months, and Stewart told us this morning that he saw them in a heated discussion downtown shortly before Jeff's death. And, according to Kate, they had some sort of falling out. Maybe whatever happened between them was Trevor's motive for murdering Jeff."

"That's true," Grace said. "Trevor could be trying to throw suspicion on Kelly, because *he* is the killer."

"Or maybe Jeff and Kelly *were* having an affair, and Rachel or Stewart killed Jeff in a moment of rage," Sam suggested.

"And even if their relationship were innocent, Stewart or Rachel could have misinterpreted it, which would still give them a perceived motive," Connie said. "I wish we could know for sure what happened between Trevor and Jeff. That could be the key to unlocking this mystery. I'm going to call Kate tomorrow to remind her to ask around. Either Jeff or Trevor had to have confided in someone. Beyond that, I'm just not sure what we can do. I feel like we've hit a dead end."

Grace looked thoughtfully at Connie and then at Sam. "It sounds like the two of you could use a break from the case. Why don't you do something fun tomorrow, and I can take care of the store. Sam, is there something you've been wanting to do while you're in southwest Florida?"

It didn't take Sam long to reply. "Isn't there a Thomas Edison and Henry Ford museum near here? I've always been intrigued by those two men."

"Yes, that's a wonderful idea," Grace said. "The *Edison and Ford Winter Estates* are in Fort Myers. You should really see that while you're in the area."

"I haven't been there in ages," Connie said. Then she hesitated. "But tomorrow's Friday, and the snowbirds are starting to pour back. The store will probably be really busy. Maybe we should go on Monday morning instead."

"I think you should go tomorrow," Grace insisted. "You could both use the break. It will only take a couple of hours, so if you go first thing in the morning, you'll be back before the store gets too busy."

"That's true," Connie said. "What do you think, Sam?"

"That sounds great to me. It will be the perfect way to get our minds off the case for a little while."

"It's settled then," Grace said. "I'll see you tomorrow when you get back. And please don't rush. I can handle the store."

Chapter 13

ON FRIDAY MORNING, Connie woke up early to the smell of bacon and eggs wafting into her bedroom. Sam was either excited about visiting the *Edison and Ford Winter Estates,* or his burnout was officially over. Hopefully, it was a little bit of both.

Connie showered, slipped into black capris and a V-neck baby blue Sapphire Beach t-shirt, and dressed up her casual outfit with a halo eclipse silver and blue necklace with matching bracelet and earrings. Then she joined Sam in the kitchen. A broad smile was plastered on his face as he filled two plates with food while glancing at Connie's laptop, which he had opened to the museum's homepage.

"I purchased two tickets for a self-guided tour so we can explore the grounds at our own pace," Sam said. "It looks like loads of fun."

"Perfect," Connie said, as she filled Ginger's bowl.

Ginger looked more interested in Sam's bacon than her own food, so Connie mixed some bacon juice into the dog's food so they could eat in peace. She filled a large mug of coffee and brought breakfast to the dining room table, where Sam joined her.

"Thanks for cooking, Sam. It smells amazing."

"My pleasure. I've been looking forward to this outing since we decided to go last night."

After they enjoyed a leisurely breakfast, Connie took their dirty dishes into the kitchen. "I'll clean up since you cooked. Then I want to call Kate to remind her to keep her ears open about Trevor."

"That sounds like a plan. While you're doing that, I'll take Ginger outside."

When Sam returned a half hour later, the kitchen was clean, and Connie was ready to go.

"I called Kate. She's going to make some phone calls today and call us if she discovers anything."

"That sounds good," Sam said. "I'm sure taking our minds off the details of the case today will help us in the long run."

They left Ginger at home and took Route 75 to Fort Myers. It was sunny and in the mid-seventies - a beautiful day to explore the twenty-plus acres that made up the winter estates of Thomas Alva Edison and Henry Ford and the adjacent botanical gardens.

On their way in, Sam asked another visitor to snap a photo of himself and Connie on either side of a statue of Edison under a colossal banyan tree. Then they started their tour.

They began by orienting themselves in the museum, which contained numerous artifacts from Edison's inventions and patents, as well as early Ford automobiles and information on the winter estates. Sam was mesmerized by the exhibits, so when Connie was finished, she relaxed in the gardens exploring the vegetation and observing butterflies. When Sam rejoined her, they crossed the street and headed for the historical buildings that made up the winter estates. They spent most of their time at the houses and at Thomas Edison's research laboratory.

They mostly walked in silence as they each let their surroundings take them on a journey through history. The beauty of the vegetation inspired Connie's soul. She snapped an array of photos of flowers and plants whose vibrant colors gave her ideas for pieces of jewelry she wanted to create. Once business slowed down after Easter, she would be grateful to have them for inspiration.

As they explored the fragrant Moonlight Garden, Connie could imagine all the family gatherings that must have happened on the grounds and in the Edison home.

Next, they walked along the Caloosahatchee River, taking the long way back to the main gift shop.

"I'm so glad we came here," Connie said. "The beauty of this place is so inspiring and uplifting."

"It reminds me that Thomas Edison was known for his perseverance," Sam said. "I once heard that he welcomed failure, because it meant he was that much closer to success."

"In that case, maybe we haven't wasted so much time trying to find Jeff's killer. It doesn't feel like we're close to victory, but who knows? Maybe we're nearer than we think. I'll bet Edison didn't feel as if he were close to inventing the light bulb until it actually happened."

"Maybe you're right. Success could be right around the corner," Sam said.

Sam purchased a small green book filled with inspirational quotations from Edison and Ford for himself and a sweatshirt for Janet, while Connie purchased a small plant for her balcony and a Christmas tree ornament that resembled an Edison bulb.

"Maybe I'll find some needed inspiration in this book," Sam said, as they walked past the old banyan tree and returned to their car.

"It can't hurt. In fact, you can't help but be inspired by these men's accomplishments."

It was just before 11:00 when they left the museum, so Connie figured she hadn't missed much in the store. On the way back to *Just Jewelry*, they stopped at Palm Paradise to pick up Ginger, then drove down Sapphire Beach Boulevard to the downtown district.

When they arrived, things were just starting to get busy for Grace, so Connie assisted customers while Grace hopped behind the check-out register. Sam naturally took it upon himself to greet everyone who came through the door. He had a special way of making people feel as if they were the only person in the world when he talked with them. Sam once again had success selling some of Connie's Fair Trade pieces.

At 2:00, Grace left for the day. She was excited to be going to the movies with Brenda, an old friend who, for years, had rented a condo in Palm Paradise during the months of January, February, and March.

Sam continued to assist Connie until Abby arrived at 4:00. Then he took Ginger for a walk around town in hopes of finding some souvenirs for Daniel and Patrick.

By the time he returned an hour later with a large pizza in hand, traffic had slowed down significantly. Until she inhaled the mingled scents of tomato sauce, veggies, and cheese, Connie hadn't realized that they skipped lunch. She had to smile as she remembered all of the times at *Feeding the Hungry* when she and Sam were working late on a project and Sam would disappear for a few minutes only to return with a veggie pizza. It was a running joke in the office that Sam had a talent for feeding the hungry in more ways than one.

Just after Connie finished her first slice of pizza, her cell phone rang.

"It's Kate," Connie said, as she wiped her hands on a napkin.

"Hi, Kate. I'm here with Sam and Abby. We seem to have a reprieve of customers, so I'm going to put you on speaker. Were you able to learn anything more about what happened between Jeff and Trevor?"

"I figured I'd go straight to the source, so I have a phone call out to Trevor. He hasn't called me back yet, but I have some other news. I was at my parents' house for lunch today and found Jeff's old high school yearbook. I was flipping through the pages and discovered something very interesting. Apparently, Stewart and Rachel were in the same graduating class. They were juniors when Jeff was a senior."

"That doesn't seem so unusual. It's a small town, after all," Connie said.

"That's true, but they were both involved in the student newspaper, so they definitely knew each other. There were a couple of photos of the two of them together, and it looked like they were friends."

Connie was silent.

"Connie, are you there?"

"I'm here. I guess it's possible that, since they knew each other in high school, and Stewart thought his wife and Rachel's husband were having an affair, he approached her to talk about it. But that still doesn't directly connect either of them to Jeff's murder."

"I agree, but I thought I'd mention it, anyway. It seemed like quite a coincidence."

"Maybe you're right. Could you arrange for us to talk with Rachel again? I think it's important to find out if Stewart told her about his suspicions. If he did, it would mean that Rachel was aware of the affair, or at least the possibility of an affair."

"Yes, I can arrange that. Are you free in the morning?" Kate asked. "Rachel is usually home on Saturday mornings."

"That would work. I'm sure Grace can cover the store for a little while."

"Perfect. I'll text you to confirm, but let's plan on meeting at *Just Jewelry* at 10:00."

Just as Connie reached for a second slice of pizza, her cell phone rang again. "It's like Grand Central Station tonight. I don't think I'm destined to get that second slice of pizza." She glanced at her phone. "It's Elyse."

"Hi, Elyse," she answered.

"Connie, I'm so glad I caught you. Are you by any chance at home?"

"No. I'm at the shop. Is everything okay?"

"I'm not sure. I just finished showing a condo in Naples. I've called Gertrude three times in the last hour, and she hasn't returned my call. It's going to take me more than a half hour to get to Palm Paradise, so I was hoping you were at home and could run up and check on her. Don't worry, I'll think of something. Forget I called. I'll try Grace."

"Grace went to the movies with a friend tonight. I doubt her cell phone is on."

"Shoot."

"You know what, it's almost closing time. Sam and I can go by and check on Gertrude. Abby can cover the store."

Abby nodded her agreement.

"It's settled," Connie said to Elyse. "We're on our way."

"Thank you! I'm leaving Naples now. Call me if you find that something is wrong. Otherwise, I'll see you in a half hour."

Connie and Sam drove back to Palm Paradise in silence and took the elevator straight to the fifth floor. Connie practically ran down the corridor to Gertrude's door.

Sam knocked loudly three times, but there was no answer.

Connie knocked again and put her ear to the door. She didn't hear anything.

"Maybe she went out," Sam said.

"Or maybe she fell and is lying unconscious on the floor. She usually answers her cell phone right away. I hate to do it, but I'm going to use the key under the door mat."

Connie slowly opened the door. "Gertrude?"

There was no reply.

"I hate to just walk in," Connie said.

"You go in alone in case she's not decent."

Connie's heart pounded as she entered Gertrude's condo. After she took a few steps, she heard a noise coming from the bathroom.

Was that music?

She motioned for Sam to follow her inside. "Wait here. I think she's in the bathroom. I'll let you know if I need any help."

Connie opened the bathroom door and found Gertrude soaking in a bubble bath bopping to sixties music, which was playing on a boom box that was sitting on the bathroom vanity.

No wonder she couldn't hear Elyse's phone calls.

"Gertrude! I'm so sorry. Elyse has been trying to call you for an hour. She was so worried that she asked me to check on you."

Connie let out a sigh of relief while Gertrude shifted around the bubbles to ensure that she was completely covered.

"Can you hand me that towel, sweetie?" she asked, pointing to a yellow towel on top of the toilet seat. "I'm just about done in here, anyway."

Connie handed Gertrude the towel. "I'll give you some privacy."

Connie shot off a quick text to Elyse. *Gertrude is fine. You'll see when you get here.*

About ten minutes later, Gertrude emerged wearing lavender silk pajamas and a black robe.

"Now, tell me, what is all this commotion about?" Gertrude asked.

Before Connie or Sam could answer, Elyse came bursting through the door. She must have driven well over the speed limit to have arrived so fast. Elyse ran up to Gertrude and hugged her tightly. "Thank goodness you're okay!" Then her relief turned to frustration. "Why didn't you answer your phone? I was terrified that something happened to you."

"Oh, honey, I love you, but you have to stop worrying so much about me. It's not good for either one of us. I was taking a nice bubble bath and listening to some music. I must have left the phone in my bedroom. I would have called you back when I got out of the tub and saw your messages."

"Since everything is okay, we'll leave you two alone," Connie said, giving Gertrude a hug.

"I'm sorry for all the trouble, Connie. You're a good neighbor and friend, even if my family is a little crazy," Gertrude said, shooting Elyse a menacing look.

Elyse hugged Connie and Sam. "Thanks, you two. I owe you big."

"Don't even mention it," Sam said. "We're just glad everything is okay."

Connie held up Gertrude's spare key. "I'll put this back under the welcome mat on the way out."

Chapter 14

ON SATURDAY MORNING, Kate picked up Connie and Sam right on time, and the three headed to Rachel's house. The last time Connie had been there was the morning after Jeff's body was discovered in his car on the side of the road. It was less than a week ago, but it felt like a month had passed. Connie and Sam brought a coffee cake they had bought at Publix that morning, so that they wouldn't show up at Rachel's empty-handed.

"Do you think Rachel has any clue that Trevor suspects Jeff of having an affair?" Connie asked Kate, as they drove to Rachel's.

"If, in fact, Trevor didn't create that story as a decoy to throw suspicion off of himself," Sam said.

"True," Connie said. "In any case, we should tread lightly. We don't want to cause Rachel any unnecessary pain. After all, it's only a theory."

Rachel seemed somewhat confused when the three of them arrived but politely invited them inside. Apparently, Kate didn't mention she was bringing friends.

Rachel offered them a cup of coffee she had just brewed, and she set some dessert plates on the kitchen table. Kate sliced the coffee cake and gave them each a healthy piece.

"Again, we're so sorry for your loss, Rachel. How are you holding up?" Connie asked.

"I guess I'm just trying to get used to my new normal, whatever that is. I think it's going to take a long time. I return to work on Monday morning. I hope that keeping busy will help."

"Rachel teaches at the Sapphire Beach Elementary School," Kate said.

Rachel smiled. "Fourth grade."

Connie warmly returned her smile. "I'm sure your students will be glad to have you back."

Rachel chuckled. "I'm not sure about that. I think they might prefer the easy pace of a substitute teacher. But like it or not, they're getting me back."

"I'm glad you have your work to throw yourself back into," Kate said. "The kids will help take your mind off things. And speaking of kids, did you hear that Tim is going to open the after-school program on Monday? Sam has agreed to help him while he's in town."

"I did hear that," Rachel said. "That's great news. Tim is coming by later this afternoon to talk about the future of the program. He asked me to make a list of all the tasks that Jeff performed for the program and any plans he had mentioned to me. Apparently, he's putting together a detailed job description for the next executive director."

Rachel studied Connie for a brief moment. Then her gaze shifted to Sam. "I appreciate that the two of you are investigating Jeff's death, but I don't understand why you aren't leaving it to the police. It seems like they are doing a thorough job. I've talked with Detective Joshua Miller several times this week already."

"Connie has helped the police solve a number of cases in the past," Kate said. "I figured it can't do any harm. I hope you don't mind, but I feel like I can't begin the grieving process until Jeff's killer is behind bars."

Rachel shifted in her seat. "I suppose if you put it that way. But I only know what I already told you. Jeff and I were watching TV last Saturday night…" She paused. "I just realized that a week ago today was the last day I spent with Jeff. We had a great day together."

Connie looked at Sam and she could tell from his expression that he had caught Rachel's slip-up, too. Jeff had specifically said that he spent the afternoon alone, because his wife was meeting an old high school friend for coffee.

Sam studied Rachel. "I don't mean to make you uncomfortable, but when I had dinner with Jeff, I distinctly remember him saying that he spent the afternoon alone. He told me you were having coffee with a friend from high school."

Rachel opened her mouth as if to speak, but no words came out.

Connie pushed aside her empty plate. "Rachel, is Stewart Robinson the old friend whom you were having coffee with last Saturday afternoon?"

Rachel's eyes flew open. She looked at Kate and then back at Connie. "Wow. You really *have* been investigating." Rachel's gaze dropped to the floor. Then she looked back at Kate, who nodded.

"It's okay. Don't worry about hurting me. Just tell them what you know."

Rachel swallowed hard. "I didn't want to mention it in front of Kate, because I didn't want her memory of her brother to be tarnished. But Stewart contacted me out of the blue last Friday. We were on the school newspaper together back in high school, but we didn't really keep in touch. We only saw each other at high school reunions and around town occasionally. Stewart told me that his son, Andy, was part of Jeff's after-school program and that Jeff had been helping his wife, Kelly, with some repairs around the house and some financial assistance. He also told me that he suspected that Jeff and Kelly were having an affair."

"It seems like it was normal for Jeff to help struggling families," Connie said.

"You're right. And that's what I told Stewart. As far as Jeff was concerned, the kids in his program were like his own kids. It wasn't uncommon for him to buy presents at Christmas for their parents to put under the tree when he knew it was a rough year or to help out with an occasional bill. He said he used money from the after-school program, but I know that wasn't possible on the program's budget. The money usually came out of his own pocket. But I don't know where he would have found enough money to pay Kelly's rent."

"Do you think he could have had an outside donor?" Kate asked.

"It's possible. Some of the members of the board of directors were wealthy. As I said, I do know that the money didn't come from our account."

"Rachel, do you believe that Jeff was unfaithful to you?" Connie asked.

"Absolutely not!" Rachel said. "I assured Stewart that Jeff would never do that. I explained that Jeff provided this type of assistance to a lot of people. He was pretty handy, and he had a huge heart."

"I can vouch for that," Kate said. "He was my go-to guy whenever I needed repairs at home or in the store. He must have saved me a fortune over the years."

"Did Stewart believe you?" Sam asked.

"No. He accused me of being naïve. He thought that was just Jeff's way of covering up his deceptive activities. Once I realized that there was no convincing him, I stopped trying. I said I would keep my eyes open, just to shut him up, but really, I think he was wrong. Our marriage was solid."

"Did Stewart seem unstable in any way?" Connie asked.

Rachel shrugged. "I don't think so. Why would you ask that?" Then Rachel's eyes flew open. "Wait! Do you think Stewart killed Jeff because he thought he was having an affair with Kelly?"

"We don't know what to think," Kate said. "As far as I know, Jeff didn't have any enemies. Who else could have done it?"

Rachel remained speechless.

"It's just one theory," Connie said. "We just wanted to ask you about it."

"You know, Stewart didn't even reach out to offer his condolences after Jeff died," Rachel said. "Maybe it *was* him."

"I don't think we should jump to any conclusions, but he is on our list of suspects," Connie said.

"There was something else we wanted to ask you," Kate said.

Rachel pushed aside her uneaten slice of coffee cake and leaned on the table. "What is it?"

"We think it could be important to find out for sure what happened between Trevor and Jeff a few months ago. They obviously had a major disagreement, and in all the years they have been friends, that's the first time I know of that they ever stopped talking. Can you think of anything at all that might give us a clue about what happened between them?"

"Jeff wouldn't talk about it, and neither would Trevor," Rachel replied. "Jeff pretended it was no big deal, but it must have been important, because it obviously damaged their friendship."

"Trevor told us the same thing," Connie said. "He also is the one who first suggested to us that Jeff was having an affair with Kelly. I hate to ask this, Rachel, but are you sure there wasn't anything between Jeff and Kelly?"

Rachel looked upset. "Oh no, not you, too. I'm telling you, Jeff wasn't that type, and things were good between us. He was *not* having an affair. Besides, Kelly came to the wake to pay her respects and there was nothing awkward about it. She was genuinely grieving his loss and told me about all he had done for her. A mistress wouldn't have been so kind to me."

"Unless she is a good actress," Kate said.

"She seemed sincere to me," Rachel said. "But it *is* really strange that Trevor would say that. He knows Jeff really well, and he knows that Jeff would never have had an affair. I can't imagine why he would have said that to you."

"Maybe he was trying to turn our attention off of himself by insinuating that Jeff had an affair," Connie suggested.

"So, now you're saying *Trevor* is the killer?" Rachel asked.

"Again, we're just exploring all possible theories," Connie said.

"I can't believe that, either. None of these suspects makes any sense to me," Rachel said.

"I agree," Kate said. "But then again, Jeff being murdered doesn't make any sense, either. So, who knows? Connie and Sam could be right."

Rachel put her head in her hands. Then she looked up at Kate. "I just can't think about this anymore. I'm sorry."

Kate scooted her chair closer to Rachel and put her arm around her shoulders. "I'm sorry, Rachel. The last thing we wanted to do was upset you."

Rachel leaned her head on Kate's shoulder. "I know. You've always had Jeff's back. I'm glad you're looking into this, because I just don't have the energy. But I don't think there is anything else I can tell you."

Kate motioned to Connie and Sam that it was time to go. "We'll leave you alone. I'm headed to my boutique for a few hours, but I'll check back in on you later to see how you're doing. Maybe I'll bring a pizza by after work."

"That sounds lovely," Rachel said. "I'll be okay. It's just a lot to process."

Connie and Kate brought their dishes and mugs into the kitchen, and Kate loaded them into the dishwasher.

"Are you sure you're going to be okay?" Kate asked. "I could skip work and come back here after I drop off Connie and Sam downtown."

Rachel forced a smile. "I'll be fine. I'm going to go for a run to work off that pizza we're going to have tonight. I also have a tub of chocolate ice cream in my freezer that has our names on it."

Kate smiled as they left. "Sounds like a plan."

Chapter 15

AS KATE BROUGHT Connie and Sam back downtown after their visit with Rachel, they discussed the case.

"I know that when someone is murdered, they say it's usually the spouse who did it," Kate said. "But I still have a hard time believing that Rachel killed my brother. And I don't think I'm being biased. I just don't see it."

"My gut tells me the same thing," Sam said. "I think Trevor was lying about Jeff's affair with Kelly to throw us off."

"Does that mean you're leaning towards Trevor as your top suspect?" Connie asked.

"Either Trevor or Stewart," Sam said. "I only met Jeff once, but I've been replaying our conversation in my mind. He expressed to me how much he appreciated the sacrifices that Rachel was making so that he could start his non-profit. He wasn't earning a lot of money, and he appreciated that she was willing to let him follow his heart. I don't think he would have betrayed her. Of course, if he had, I can see how it would have thrown Rachel into a fit of rage given all the sacrifices she made to make him happy."

"If that's true, and I tend to agree with you, then Kelly wouldn't have had a motive to kill him, either," Connie said.

"But we know that Stewart *believed* Kelly and Jeff were having an affair, so that still leaves him on the table as a suspect," Kate said.

"And we also know that Stewart has no alibi. He was supposed to take Andy on Saturday night, but he canceled, because he was sick. That seems suspicious to me."

"On the other hand, Trevor seems to have been sending us on a wild goose chase with Kelly," Sam said. "He looks every bit as guilty as Stewart, and he doesn't have an alibi, either. He was alone at home while his wife was in Immokalee."

Connie watched the palm trees fly by from the back seat of Kate's car. "We need more information. It's more important than ever that we talk to Trevor. We need to ask him directly what his disagreement with Jeff was about."

"But we already asked him, and he lied to us," Sam said. "He told us that his disagreement with Jeff was over his affair with Kelly. What makes you think he would tell us the truth if we asked him again?"

"Besides, he hasn't returned my call," Kate said. "I think he's avoiding me because he knows we're investigating."

"I guess we'll have to be more persistent. It's a crucial piece of information that we don't yet have, and I still believe it's the key to solving this case," Connie said.

"I have an idea," Kate said. "I'm friends with Trevor's wife, Justine. Maybe she knows something. It would probably be easier to get it out of her than Trevor."

"If Jeff didn't tell Rachel what their disagreement was about, what makes you think Trevor told Justine?" Sam asked.

"I say it's worth a shot," Connie said. "We don't have any other option. Kate, do you think you could arrange for us to talk to her?"

"I don't see why not. Justine and I usually have lunch together once a month. Sometimes Rachel joins us, but with everything Rachel is going through, I doubt she'd come, even if I invited her."

"How are *you* doing, Kate? You're worried about Rachel, but this must be heart-wrenching for you, as well. Would it be easier if Sam and I talked to Justine alone?"

Kate swallowed hard. "I think Justine would be more willing to talk if I were with you. And thanks for your concern, but as hard as it is, investigating Jeff's death is helping me feel like I'm at least doing something useful. I don't have the heart to throw myself back into my work yet, so getting justice for my brother is the only thing that seems to bring me any semblance of peace these days."

"Okay," Sam said. "Just promise you will let us know if it gets too difficult."

"I promise," Kate said as she parallel parked on the street in front of *Just Jewelry.*

"Let us know when you can arrange a meeting with Trevor's wife," Connie called out as she exited the car.

"Will do."

It was 10:45 when they returned to the store, well before the Saturday afternoon rush. Sam took Connie's car and went back to Palm Paradise to spend the afternoon at the pool, so Connie was free to focus on work.

As she anticipated, it was a busy day. Grace stayed a little later, so Connie wouldn't be alone for too long. This was the second January that Connie had been in business, and, fortunately, it was even busier than last year, as word spread about the quality of her jewelry. It was a good problem to have, especially since she had just taken on a mortgage to purchase the building that housed her shop. But she still hated the idea of her employees picking up the slack. She definitely had to hire someone else. She promised herself that she would focus on hiring another part-time employee, as soon as Sam went back to Massachusetts and Jeff's murder was solved.

An hour later, Abby arrived. Around dinnertime, it started to slow down, and Connie noticed that she had a text message on her phone from Kate.

Justine is free to meet for lunch tomorrow at 1:00. Will that work for you and Sam?

Shoot. That meant she would have to leave Grace alone in the store on a Sunday during the busiest time of the day.

Any chance we could meet a little earlier? Connie replied. *Would noon work? We could eat at* Gallagher's Tropical Shack.

A few minutes later there was a response from Kate. *I just checked with Justine and noon works for us. We'll see you at* Gallagher's.

Connie felt better about their plans. She would hopefully be back in the shop before the afternoon rush, and if she saw things getting busy from *Gallagher's,* she could always excuse herself, and Sam and Kate could talk to Justine without her.

As the evening wore on, the downtown streets emptied out.

"If you'd like to spend some more time with Sam, I can take it from here," Abby said. "I don't think we'll have many more customers tonight."

"Thanks, Abby. I think I will. I appreciate the extra hours you're putting in, but I know your schedule will get tighter once spring classes begin. I've decided that as soon as Sam leaves, I'm going to make it a priority to hire another part-time employee. If you know of anyone, please let me know."

"A few extra hours here and there don't bother me," Abby said. "But I think that's a good idea for your own well-being. I'll give it some thought and let you know."

Just before she was about to leave, Elyse came into the store looking deflated.

"Can I get you a cup of coffee, Elyse?" Connie asked. "You look exhausted."

"No thanks. I just stopped in for a minute. I wanted to thank you and Sam again for checking on Gertrude last night."

"No problem at all. I'm glad everything turned out okay. How did it go after we left?"

Elyse threw both hands into the air in surrender. "I give up. I don't know what I'm going to do with that woman. She is the most ornery person I have ever met."

"She is a tough one," Connie said. "But that's part of her charm."

Elyse put her hands on her hips. "There is nothing charming about her stubbornness. It's going to be the death of me."

"Tell me what happened," Connie said, guiding Elyse to the seating area. Elyse plopped down in the armchair, and Connie sat on the couch facing her.

"The whole reason I was calling her last night was because I wanted to stop by after work to give her some information on a medical alert system. It's a discreet white bracelet with a button she could press if she needed help."

"Let me guess. Gertrude wanted no part of it."

"She wouldn't even look at the brochure. She insisted that the problem was all in our imaginations. She said that if everyone around her hadn't overreacted at the slightest issue, there would be no problem. She insisted that indigestion and a bubble bath do not indicate a need for a medical alert system." Elyse shook her head. "She told us that those contraptions are for old people, not healthy, active eighty-eight year-olds."

Connie unsuccessfully tried to stop herself from laughing.

After a few seconds Elyse also burst out in laughter.

"I suppose it *is* funny," Elyse continued, "but it's also maddening. Connie, I'm so worried about her. It's true that none of these things turned out to be an actual emergency, but they easily could have. I can't make her understand how stressful it is for her family. If for no other reason, she should wear it for our peace of mind."

"I see your problem," Connie said. "Is there another way to keep an eye on her? Maybe Grace and I could make it a point to stop by more often."

"That's nice of you, but..." Elyse's voice trailed off in thought. "Wait a minute. You just gave me an idea. There is a super sweet gentleman in his seventies named Burt who lives next door to Gertrude. He sometimes brings her food when he cooks, and she does the same. What if my parents and I offered to pay him in return for checking in with Gertrude every day? It's not ideal, but at least it would somewhat ease my mind."

"I don't know, Elyse. Gertrude would be furious with you if she ever found out. I wouldn't want to be in a one-hundred-mile radius if she did."

Elyse raised her eyebrows and smiled mischievously. "I guess we have to make sure she never finds out then." She hopped up from her chair with renewed energy. "I'm going to call my parents and see what they think."

"And I'm going to pretend I don't know anything about this," Connie said.

Connie walked out with Elyse since she was planning to leave, anyway.

When Connie returned to Palm Paradise, she found a sun-tanned Sam and a sleepy Ginger snuggled on the couch watching a police procedural movie. Ginger looked content with her head on Sam's lap. Connie hoped her furry friend wouldn't miss Sam too much after he left next week.

"Did you eat dinner yet?" Connie asked. "I was going to heat myself up some leftovers."

"Yes, Ginger and I ate when I got back from the pool. Then we went for a nice walk through some of the side streets that run perpendicular to the boulevard. Everyone is so friendly here." Sam yawned. "Between the sunshine, the walking, and the fresh air, I'm going to sleep well tonight."

"A day in the sun has that effect on me, too."

"I was surprised that I was the only one at the pool today," Sam said.

Connie chuckled. "Seventy degrees is considered cold here and not pool weather by many of the locals' standards, especially when there's a breeze coming off the gulf."

"Their loss was my gain," Sam said. "It was like being at a private pool."

Connie filled Sam in on Elyse's plan for Gertrude and their lunch plans with Kate and Justine the following day.

"I hope Justine knows more than Rachel does," Sam said. "And I sure hope Elyse's plan doesn't backfire."

"You and me both."

Chapter 16

AFTER MASS ON SUNDAY morning, Fr. Paul Fulton was standing in the church vestibule, greeting parishioners as they exited. Connie started to introduce him to Sam, but the two men informed her that they had already chatted the week before when Sam attended Mass with Grace.

"Don't hold it against Fr. Paul that it was one of his homilies that convinced me to stay in Sapphire Beach and open *Just Jewelry*," Connie said playfully to Sam.

"Now, don't go telling this fine gentleman something like that. He might take back whatever money he put in the collection basket."

Sam laughed. "If I'm honest, deep down I knew I would lose Connie sooner or later. I'm glad she found her way to such a wonderful community."

After Mass, Connie and Sam swung by the condo to pick up Ginger, and then they headed downtown. They took her for a leisurely walk around town before opening the store, as was Connie's usual habit. Connie liked to take advantage of the peaceful Sunday mornings to give Ginger some exercise and mentally prepare for the day.

An hour and a half later, Grace arrived with three coffees, and they chatted in the store's seating area until customers began to trickle in.

"Are you sure you don't mind Sam and me taking off for lunch?" Connie asked. "I feel like I've been abandoning you and Abby too much lately."

"Don't be crazy. I enjoy keeping busy, and besides, you'll be back for the biggest part of the rush."

"I'll keep an eye on the store from *Gallagher's,* and if it looks like it's getting too busy for one person to manage, I'll come right over. And promise you'll text me if you need me."

Grace raised her right hand. "I swear."

A couple of minutes before noon, Connie and Sam crossed the street to *Gallagher's Tropical Shack*. As they climbed the wooden stairs, Kate called out to Connie and Sam from behind. "I just love this restaurant. The surfboards mounted on the driftwood wall and the thatched roof make me feel like I'm in the Caribbean."

Connie agreed. "I have a view of the thatched roof from my shop, and every time I glance over, I feel like I'm on a tropical island."

Kate reintroduced Connie, Sam, and Justine, since they had already briefly met at Jeff's funeral reception, and the party of four was seated near the front window.

"This is perfect," Connie said. "I can keep an eye on my shop."

"Is Gallagher here?" Connie asked the hostess who seated them.

She shook her head and smiled. "He took the day off to spend it with Stephanie."

Connie was thrilled that Gallagher had shifted his priorities. Last year, Gallagher worked non-stop and would never have considered taking a Sunday off during tourist season.

Kate pulled out a navy blue sun dress from a bag she was carrying. "We did a little shopping before lunch. What do you think?"

"It's lovely," Connie said. "The color is perfect for you."

"Kate said you had some questions for me related to Jeff's death," Justine said, after they ordered lunch. "I wish I could help you, but I have no idea who would have wanted to hurt him. Jeff and Rachel were good friends to Trevor and me, and as far as I know, Jeff didn't have any enemies. It was actually quite the opposite. Everybody in town admired him for what he was doing with his after-school program."

"That's what we're learning," Connie said.

Sam glanced around the restaurant, and his eyes settled on a table on the other side of the room.

"Is everything okay, Sam?" Kate asked.

Sam forced a smile. "I just realized that the last time I was in this restaurant, I was with Jeff. It was the night he died." He pointed to a table near the bar. "We were sitting right there."

"What a terrible way to begin your vacation," Justine said.

"I suppose you could look at it that way. But I'm glad to have had the chance to meet him. Jeff reminded me of myself when I was starting out in the non-profit sector. I think our conversation helped me to remember my initial passion for the work we do."

Kate smiled at Sam. "It's wonderful to hear that."

Connie directed the conversation back to their reason for being there. "Justine, we were hoping you might be able to tell us what happened between Trevor and Jeff a few months ago."

"They had been friends since college," Kate added, "and I've never known them to have a serious disagreement."

Justine shrugged her shoulders. "I really couldn't say. I'm sure they would have made up eventually. It couldn't have been anything important, or Trevor would have told me. Personally, I think they were together so much that they needed a break. You know how it can be with close friends. They spent a lot of their free time together, then Trevor volunteered in the after-school program. Rachel and I talked about it on the phone the other night, and we think they just needed some time apart. They were probably getting on one another's nerves."

The server delivered their sandwiches, and Connie loaded her fries with ketchup. "Did Trevor ever mention to you that he suspected Jeff was having an affair?"

Justine's eyes flew wide open, and she nearly choked on her burger. "Of course not. Why would you ask that?"

"We ran into Trevor when we went to Rachel's house to offer our condolences, and while we were walking back to our cars, Trevor told us he thought Jeff might be having an affair with the mother of one of the kids from the after-school program," Connie said.

"Someone also saw Trevor and Jeff together having a heated discussion just a few days before Jeff's death," Sam added.

Justine leaned back in her chair. "I have no idea why Trevor would say something like that. He, of all people, should know that Jeff would never cheat on Rachel." Justine paused, then her eyes flew open again. "Wait a minute! You don't suspect Trevor of killing Jeff, do you? Is that why you're asking about their disagreement?"

Just as Connie opened her mouth to reply, Justine's cell phone rang. She took it from her purse and glanced at the screen. "The caller ID says Gulf Coast Medical Center. I'd better answer it."

Justine stepped outside to take the call.

Connie watched her pace the sidewalk as she listened to whomever she was speaking with. The concern on Justine's face quickly turned to horror. After a couple of minutes, Justine rushed back inside the restaurant.

"Is everything okay?" Kate asked.

Clearly, it was not.

"It was the hospital. Trevor was brought into the emergency room in an ambulance a half hour ago. He was hit by a car while bicycling. He told the doctor that someone tried to run him off the road. I need to go to him right away."

Kate stood abruptly. "I'll take you. You don't look like you're in any condition to drive."

Justine grabbed her wallet from her purse, but Connie stopped her before she could open it. "You two just go. We'll take care of this."

"Thank you," Kate said. "We'll keep you posted."

"Well, that was disturbing," Connie said after the women left. "What do you suppose happened to Trevor?"

"I don't know, but it doesn't sound good. I guess we'll have to wait until we hear from Kate to find out."

They quickly finished their sandwiches and paid the bill, then returned to *Just Jewelry*.

"That was a fast lunch," Grace said when they walked through the door. She turned to some customers on the other side of the store. "Just let me know if I can help you with anything."

"Our lunch was interrupted when Justine received a phone call from someone at the Gulf Coast Medical Center. Apparently, Trevor was taken to the emergency room where he told a doctor that someone tried to run him off the road while he was biking."

"Oh, my!" Grace said. "Was he seriously injured?"

"That's all we know for now," Sam said. "Kate and Justine are on their way to the hospital, and Kate promised to keep us posted."

"I wasn't planning to stay here all afternoon," Sam said. "But now, I think I'll stick around. I want to be here when Kate calls."

A steady stream of customers kept them busy all afternoon, and before Connie knew it, Grace had left for the day and Abby had arrived for her shift. They finally had a chance to catch their breath around dinnertime.

"You've been quite the trooper," Connie said to Sam, when she finally had a moment to sit down. "You didn't have to hang out here all afternoon."

Connie brewed a pot of strong iced tea for a much-needed late afternoon pick-me-up.

"I think I sold a necklace. I'm still waiting for my commission check for my other sales," Sam joked.

As they were finishing their iced tea, Kate, Justine, and Trevor came in.

Connie and Sam both stood at the same time.

"Trevor," Connie said, "how are you feeling? What happened?" Except for a few small bandages on his arms and legs, he looked okay physically, but the expression on his face told her something was wrong.

"Is there somewhere we could talk in private?" Trevor asked.

"I can cover the store if you want to go for a walk," Abby offered.

Connie glanced at the street through one of her front display windows. "Maybe that's a good idea. There are still a fair amount of people out and about. We won't have any privacy here."

Connie, Sam, Trevor, Justine, and Kate walked in the direction of the beach and found a couple of benches where they were out of earshot.

When they sat down, Trevor opened his mouth to speak, but nothing came out.

"Go ahead," Justine said. "Tell Connie what you told us."

Trevor inhaled deeply. "First, I want to apologize for sending you down the wrong path when I told you that Jeff was having an affair with Kelly Robinson. I thought if you hit some dead ends, you'd give up the investigation."

"Why would you want us to give up the investigation?" Connie asked. "Don't you want to know what happened to your friend?"

Trevor looked away. When he returned his gaze to Connie and Sam, his eyes were moist.

"I think I already know what happened to him," Trevor said.

"Why wouldn't you tell the police if you knew who killed Jeff?" Connie asked Trevor. "Who are you trying to protect?"

"Myself."

Chapter 17

CONNIE'S HEART FELT like it would pound through her chest. She scooted closer to Sam, who was seated next to her.

"Don't worry, Connie," Justine said. "It's not what it sounds like."

Trevor rested his arm on the back of the bench behind Justine. "Let me start from the beginning. A few months ago, our friend Bill quit the after-school program's board of directors before his term was up."

"I remember," Connie said. "He quit because his career as an art dealer was taking off. But I didn't realize he left in the middle of a term."

"He did. And Jeff was furious. He was counting heavily on Bill's continued support and expertise.

Jeff felt betrayed. He took it as an attack on his kids. Jeff told me that he always believed he could count on Bill, even though they had ultimately taken different paths in life. Jeff, Bill, and I all met on a spring break service trip during our freshman year in college. At the time, we all had a passion for service, but over the years, Bill's priorities shifted, especially once he married Audrey. I told him to forget about it - that people change - but he wouldn't."

"What do you mean?" Sam asked. "Was he just angry, or did he take action?"

Trevor ran his hand through his light brown hair. "Jeff was the kind of guy who took everyone's problems upon himself."

Sam smirked in Connie's direction. "Sounds like someone I know."

Connie pretended to push Sam away. "Now look who's calling the kettle black. Sorry, Trevor. Please continue."

"As you know, many of the kids in the after-school program come from families who are struggling financially, and Jeff was always doing what he could to help them. And as I'm sure you know by now, that's what he was doing at Kelly's, as he had done for many others."

Kate nodded. "I don't think I realized the extent of it until all those people came up to Rachel and me at the wake and told us that Jeff had been helping their families financially or with home repairs," Kate said. "But we didn't know where he got the money from. Tim said it didn't come from the program's budget, and Rachel said it didn't come from their personal bank account, either."

"I remember," Connie said. "Trevor, do you know where he got it?"

"I'm getting to that. Bill had a tendency to drink a little too much. I wouldn't call him an alcoholic, but when he drinks, he starts bragging and talking about himself. He completely loses his filter, if you know what I mean. He can be obnoxious."

So that was why Audrey stopped Bill from drinking at the funeral reception.

"Anyway," Trevor continued, "one night, after a few too many, Bill let it slip that he was making a hefty amount of money through unethical means. Apparently, he was selling artwork on the black market."

"Bill insisted that he could get me a good deal on artwork, but I didn't realize he was talking about *that* good of a deal," Sam said.

Trevor nodded. "Both Jeff and I were taken aback when Bill told us this. We knew he was becoming more and more shallow, but we didn't imagine he was involved in illegal activity. One night, after a long day of talking to parents and listening to their problems, Jeff hatched an idea. He started blackmailing Bill for cash, which he would, in turn, give to families in need."

"So, that's how he paid Kelly's rent and helped the others?" Sam asked. "By playing Robin Hood?"

"Pretty much. In some strange way, Jeff thought it was the right thing to do. And he saw it as an added benefit that he could stick it to Bill for quitting the board mid-term. I'm ashamed to say that, at first, I didn't see any harm in it. But, of course, as you know, there is always someone in need. After the third time that Jeff blackmailed Bill, he said he wasn't going to give Jeff any more money, and he threatened him. At that point, I got scared and told Jeff that if he didn't stop, I wouldn't spend any more time with him. I wanted to distance myself from Jeff, because I was afraid Bill might follow through with his threat to Jeff and hurt me and my family, as well."

"Is that what you and Jeff were talking about downtown a few days before he died?" Connie asked. "Stewart saw the two of you in a heated discussion."

"Yes," Trevor said. "I tried one last time to convince Jeff to stop blackmailing Bill. I was afraid he'd get hurt, and it looks like my fears were grounded. I can't prove it, but I'm convinced Bill killed Jeff, and he was sending me a message this morning to keep quiet about it by running me off the road."

"Did you see Bill driving the car that hit you?" Connie asked.

"Not exactly, but I think I saw a white car speeding away, and Bill has a white BMW. At least, I *think* that was the car that pushed me off the road. I was listening to music, so the whole thing took me by surprise. By the time I knew what was happening, I was focused on staying alive."

"I've told Trevor a million times to take out his earbuds while he rides his bike," Justine said.

Trevor shrugged. "I know. But it helps me unwind. I was on a residential street, so I thought I would be safe."

"Why would Bill feel the need to threaten you now?" Sam asked. "Did something happen between the two of you recently?"

"Kind of," Trevor said. "My conscience has been bothering me every time I see Rachel or Kate. They deserved to know what happened to Jeff. So, I confronted Bill yesterday and asked him to look me in the eye and tell me he didn't kill Jeff. He pretended to look hurt, and he swore up and down that he would never do that. I can't believe how convincingly he was able to lie straight to my face."

"It seems to me that if Bill were trying to kill you, he would have succeeded," Connie said.

Trevor nodded. "I agree. I think he was sending me a warning. Things have been even more tense between us since Jeff's death. He knows that I know what happened, even though he denied it."

"Trevor, I know you're afraid of Bill, but you have to tell the police what happened," Connie said.

"I know. Justine made me promise to call them as soon as we get home. We came here on our way back from the hospital because we thought you and Sam deserved to know the truth. You've done so much to try to help Kate. Connie, I never thought I'd be saying this about one of my oldest friends, but Bill is dangerous. I could have been seriously injured this morning. Or worse. You and Sam should lay low until the police arrest him."

"Trevor is right," Kate said. "I'd never forgive myself if anything happened to the two of you. Promise me you'll stop investigating."

"It sounds like we don't need to," Connie said. "Hopefully, the police will arrest Bill soon, and this whole nightmare will be over."

After making Connie and Sam promise one more time to lay low until Bill was arrested, Trevor, Justine, and Kate left, and Connie and Sam walked back to *Just Jewelry*.

"How'd it go?" Abby asked when they returned.

They relayed the whole story to Abby.

"Well, that's a relief," Abby said. "I'm glad Trevor is going to call the police. It sounds like the case is solved. Now Sam can enjoy the rest of his vacation in peace."

"You're right," Sam said. "Now I can focus on helping Tim with the after-school program. I'm looking forward to it tomorrow. Tim texted me earlier to let me know he finished my background check, and I'm all cleared to volunteer. I think I'll head back to Palm Paradise and rest up. This has been enough excitement for one day. Connie, just text me when you're ready to leave, and I'll come back to pick you up."

"Don't be silly," Abby said, practically pushing them out the door. "I've got things under control here. The two of you should enjoy the evening."

"It would be nice to go home and unwind," Connie said.

When they got home, Connie cooked some pork chops while Sam tossed a salad, and they ate on the balcony. It was already dark, and the temperature had dropped, but Sam insisted on being outdoors as much as possible before heading back north, so Connie threw on some jeans and a fleece sweatshirt and joined Sam outside.

After they finished eating, they watched TV for a little while, then called it a night.

Chapter 18

THE BEGINNING OF SAM'S second week in Sapphire Beach was relatively uneventful. Trevor had told the police about Jeff blackmailing Bill, but so far, they hadn't made an arrest.

On Monday, Tuesday, and Wednesday, after all the children were picked up from the after-school program, Sam spent some extra time with Tim helping him draft the new executive director job description and brainstorming on the future of the organization. The next board meeting was scheduled for the following Thursday night, and Tim wanted to be prepared so plans could move forward as quickly as possible.

Sam seemed to come alive, and he finally looked like the old energetic Sam whom Connie knew and loved. Apparently, Janet was right. Two weeks in Sapphire Beach was exactly what he needed, even if she hadn't meant for his vacation to include entertaining children and investigating a murder.

Mondays and Tuesdays were typically her slowest days in the shop, so Connie took advantage of the time to schedule some social media posts and advertising and to finish up a bracelet that matched a necklace and pair of earrings, which she had made before Christmas.

On Thursday at noon, Connie took Ginger for a walk and went to a nearby sandwich shop to pick up lunch for her and Grace. She got them each a mozzarella, tomato, and basil sandwich on a French roll with a bag of popcorn and they took turns eating while the other tended to customers.

After lunch, Gallagher came over with a white paper bag, which he handed to Connie. "I saw you walking into your store with a sandwich bag, so I thought you and Grace might want to sample today's dessert special after you ate."

"You're the best, Gallagher," Connie said, opening the bag and finding two healthy slices of chocolate cheesecake.

"Wow," Grace said, "you really *are* the best. I can't wait to dig in."

"I heard you and Sam were in the restaurant yesterday," Gallagher said.

"We were. And we heard that you took the day off to spend it with Stephanie."

Gallagher smiled broadly. "We went to the beach and then out to dinner. It was a great day."

A smile spread across Grace's face, as well.

Connie had a feeling it was the fact that things seemed to be progressing between her daughter and Gallagher that made her happy, not the chocolate cheesecake, which she had just tasted.

After she finished dessert, Connie opened her laptop and started gathering her year-end financial paperwork, which she diligently worked on until Grace left. Abby arrived a couple of hours later, and Connie continued her paperwork.

At 5:00, Connie was tired of staring at the computer screen, so she closed her laptop and slid it into its carrying case. Then she went out back to heat some water to make tea for her and Abby.

About a half hour later, Sam parked Connie's silver Jetta in front of *Just Jewelry* and made a beeline for Connie, who was seated at the oak table.

"I didn't expect to see you until later tonight," Connie said. "I thought you would still be helping Tim prepare for next week's board meeting."

"That was the plan, but today Tim and I got to talking, and I learned something interesting that I wanted to tell you right away."

Abby joined them at the table.

"What did you learn?" Connie asked.

"As you know, I've had the chance to get acquainted with Tim over the past three days, and I've grown to admire him. He has a heart of gold and is committed to ensuring that Jeff's after-school program continues to thrive. He hadn't heard about what happened to Trevor on Sunday, so I ended up telling him that we thought the police would likely make an arrest soon. I didn't feel it was my place to tell him about Jeff's blackmailing scheme, but I did mention that we thought Bill was the killer. I probably shouldn't have mentioned Bill, but I wanted Tim to know that the case was close to being solved. Anyway, you won't believe what he told me."

"The suspense is killing me," Connie said. "What did he say?"

"He said that Bill couldn't have killed Jeff, because the night Jeff was killed, Bill was in a bar drinking."

"How does Tim know that?"

"Apparently, he and his wife, Lucy, were planning to go to the same bar that Bill was at, but then they walked in and saw Bill drinking alone. Tim knew that Bill was not fun to be around when he was drinking, so they left before Bill could see them."

"Wait a minute," Connie said. "That means that..."

"That means that Bill and Audrey were lying when they alibied each other. Why would Bill make up a false alibi if he already had one?"

"Maybe because he was alone," Connie said. "If it was a busy Saturday night, the bartender might not remember him, and if he paid with cash, he'd have no proof that he was actually there."

"That could be," Sam said. "But if Bill didn't kill Jeff, then who did?"

Connie ran a hand through her dark hair. "Oh, no," Connie said. "That means we're back at square one."

"I'm so sorry, guys," Abby said.

Sam smiled playfully at Connie. "I guess we need to take our cue from our new friends."

"Which new friends are you talking about?" Connie asked.

"Good old Thomas Alva Edison and Henry Ford. We need to persevere."

Connie rolled her eyes, but she and Abby couldn't help but laugh.

"I suppose you're going to tell me that ruling out all of our suspects is actually a good thing," Connie said.

"You got it. We must be close to the truth now!"

"I've really missed your corny sense of humor and your undying optimism," Connie said.

Sam grabbed the edge of the table with both hands in an overdramatic attempt to brace himself. "Did you just admit out loud to missing my jokes?"

"You can't prove a thing, Sam O'Neil. I'll deny I ever said it."

"I'm too wound up to leave now," Sam said. "Even if it means taking more abuse from you, I think I'll stick around for tonight's jewelry-making class. I enjoyed chatting with your students last week."

"If the two of you want to leave, I can teach the class," Abby volunteered. "It's good practice for when I become a professor."

"That's sweet, Abby, but it will be easier with two of us. It's a beautiful evening, and I'm guessing we'll get some customers tonight. How about if I handle the customers while you polish your teaching skills?"

Abby responded with two thumbs up.

The first student to arrive was Gertrude. Connie greeted her with a warm hug and apologized again for intruding on her bubble bath on Friday night.

"Don't even mention that," Gertrude said. "I really do appreciate that you care enough to come downstairs to check on me."

Connie decided not to mention that she had left work early to come over. Elyse might never hear the end of that. Instead, she replied by saying, "I know you would do the same for me."

Connie had a different group of students this week than last week, so she decided they would make the same sea glass bracelet to use up the beads.

Abby started class with a brief demonstration on how to begin the bracelet, and once the class got underway, the students began chatting. Connie lingered around the oak table to lend Abby a helping hand in between ringing up the occasional customer.

"I have what is turning into a big problem, and I'm not sure what I should do about it," Gertrude said, once she had settled into a rhythm with her bracelet.

"Trouble in Palm Paradise?" Lilly, who was another student, asked.

"Something like that," Gertrude said. "You won't believe it, but remember how I told you about the nice gentleman, Burt, who lives next door from me?"

At the mention of Burt's name, Connie glanced at Sam.

Lilly nodded. "You said that you enjoyed his company."

"Well, yes, I did. That is, when he only stopped by a couple of days per week. When one of us would cook, we would bring the other over some of what we made, and we would chat for a while."

"That sounds nice," Lilly said. "My neighbors are all grumps."

"Well, ever since the weekend, he's been coming over every single night to see if I need anything. On Sunday, he brought chicken over.

On Monday, he stopped by to introduce me to his buddy, who was visiting. On Tuesday, he came to tell me about a movie on TV that he thought I might enjoy. And last night, he came over with his tools, asking if I had anything that needed repairs."

"That does seem like a bit much," Lilly said. "Maybe he's sweet on you."

"I'm glad you said that Lilly, because I was thinking the same thing."

"Do you like him in that way?" Lilly asked.

Gertrude stopped working and looked at Lilly with wide eyes. "Heavens, no. At my age?"

"Why not?" Lilly asked.

"You have to be joking. I was married once, and one man is enough for one lifetime. I don't need to be changing my lifestyle now to suit some gentleman. I enjoy my freedom, and I'm not giving it up for Burt or anyone else," Gertrude insisted. "Besides, can you imagine if we became a couple? We would be Burt and Gert."

Connie and Sam both turned their heads so Gertrude wouldn't see them holding back their laughter.

"Well, then, I guess if he continues to pop by like that, you'll have to have a heart-to-heart. He seems like a nice man. I'm sure he'll understand," Lilly said.

"I guess you're right. I'd rather not have to do that, but it might be the only way out of this mess."

"I would give it a few more days," Lilly said. "Didn't you just spend the night in the hospital? Maybe it's just his way of showing you he's concerned."

"That's a good point. I'll wait a little while longer, but if he doesn't stop next week, Burt and Gert are going to have an honest conversation."

Sam stood up and walked discreetly over to Connie. "I think you'd better call Elyse right away," he whispered. "I'll let you know if you're needed out front."

Connie nodded and disappeared into the storeroom, where she would be out of earshot, and called Elyse.

"Hi Connie. How are you?" Elyse said in a cheerful voice.

Before Connie could answer, Elyse continued talking. "I think I solved the problem with Aunt Gertrude. Burt was super sweet and agreed to check in on her every day. He wouldn't even accept any payment in return. I can't tell you what a load off my mind that is."

Connie hated to burst Elyse's bubble, but she had no choice. She relayed to her friend Gertrude's conversation with Lilly.

For a few seconds there was silence on the other end of the phone. Then Elyse sighed. "I should have known it was too good to be true. Thanks for letting me know, Connie. I'll run by Burt's condo right now and let him know that the plan is off."

Chapter 19

AFTER SHE HUNG UP with Elyse, Connie straightened up the checkout area and listened as Sam chatted away with another student. Sam could find common interests with literally anyone. He was showing Joan, a woman who took Connie's classes from time to time, how to download the app for her husband's favorite pizza shop. He had convinced her that it would be easier to order takeout online rather than calling when she wanted to pick up a pizza on the way home.

Connie walked to the table.

"That's nice of you to pick up dinner, Joan," Connie said.

Joan laughed. "After forty years of marriage, Al is still helpless in the kitchen. But I don't mind. Maybe that's the secret to our long marriage. We still enjoy taking care of each other. He's changing the oil in my car tonight."

"You're both very blessed," Connie said.

Joan smiled at Connie. "Your Zach seems like that kind of guy, too. I'm sure he'll be doing things to make your life easier, after you've been married for forty years."

Connie felt her cheeks grow warm.

"Oh, I've seen the way you look at each other," Joan continued. "I'm sure you'll be together for as long as Al and me."

Sam smiled as well and playfully punched Connie's shoulder. "I tend to agree. Maybe Connie and Zach will give my wife and me a good reason to return to Sapphire Beach sometime in the near future."

Since class was nearly over, Connie washed out the coffee pot, which Abby had used earlier to brew some decaf coffee with some cookies they had bought to serve to the class. Connie loved that the large oak table that they used for making jewelry made it feel as though she were entertaining friends in her dining room, especially when it held Italian cookies and coffee.

As Connie was rinsing out the coffee pot, she thought about Trevor and how he was so sure that Bill had killed Jeff. He even thought he saw Bill's white BMW speeding away as he was tumbling over.

Suddenly, another theory about Jeff's murder that she hadn't yet considered formulated in her mind, and she nearly dropped the glass pot.

"Sam, could you come here for a minute?" Connie asked, trying to sound as normal as possible. But her mouth felt as if it had gone completely dry.

Sam excused himself from his conversation with Joan, who was thanking him profusely for setting up the app.

"What is it?" Sam asked.

"Do you still have the information that Bill gave you about the art exhibit he invited you to this weekend? I believe it started tonight."

Sam took his wallet out of his pocket and pulled out the business card that Bill had written the information on. "Here it is. The exhibit goes until 9:00. Were you in the mood for viewing art tonight?"

"No, but I think I know who killed Jeff."

Connie left a dumbfounded Sam in the back room and went to inform Abby that she would be closing the store by herself, after all.

Within five minutes, Connie and Sam were on their way to *Sheffield Art Gallery*. Connie quickly dropped off Ginger at home, since it was unlikely that they would make it back to the store before closing time. The gallery was a mile down Sapphire Beach Boulevard, in the opposite direction from downtown, so they had to pass Palm Paradise, anyway.

While she was upstairs, she texted Zach. *I think I know who killed Jeff. Can you meet Sam and me at the* Sheffield Art Gallery *ASAP?*

Before Zach could respond, they were on their way to the gallery.

Connie felt badly for the havoc she was about to wreak in Bill's life, but what else could she do?

"Aren't you going to tell me who you think the killer is?" Sam asked.

"Not until I know for sure if I'm right," Connie said. "But don't worry. I think I know how I can prove it."

While they were driving, a text came through on Connie's phone. She didn't want to take her eyes off the road, so she handed it to Sam.

"Hopefully, it's from Zach. I asked him if he'd meet us at the gallery. Can you check for me?"

"Yup. Zach says to stay out of trouble. He's on his way."

"Awesome!"

Connie glanced down at the clothes she was wearing, then at Sam's, and she realized they were both a bit underdressed.

Sam must have picked up on what she was thinking. "We probably should have changed."

"It's too late now. Let's just try to lay low as best we can until Zach gets there."

Connie didn't see Zach's car in the parking lot when they arrived, but they decided to go in, anyway.

They viewed some of the artwork and were soon spotted by Bill, who was standing next to his wife, Audrey, schmoozing with guests. Bill was talking up Thomas Carmichael, a local artist whose work was on exhibit that evening.

It didn't take long for Bill to notice Connie and Sam, and, just as he was coming over to greet them, Zach arrived. He stood next to Connie and kissed her hello.

"I'm sorry that we're a bit underdressed," Connie said to Bill. "We almost forgot that the exhibit was tonight, and Sam didn't want to miss it, so we came right from my shop."

"Don't be silly. I'm so glad you all made it," Bill said. "Detective Hughes, I didn't realize you were an art connoisseur."

Bill's eyes darted back and forth between Zach and Sam. Connie wondered if he was concerned that Zach might be onto his black market dealings. But he managed to play it cool.

"I guess you could say that Connie recently piqued my interest," Zach said.

Audrey was talking with a couple, but she appeared to be straining to hear the conversation among Connie and her group. When she finally managed to break away, she came over and stood next to Bill, just as Connie was hoping she'd do.

"How are you, Audrey?" Connie asked.

"I thought that was you and Sam. Detective Hughes, what a pleasant surprise. Thank you all for coming out to support Mr. Carmichael."

"It's our pleasure," Sam said. "Bill was right. He is incredibly talented."

"Well, if you'd like to purchase something, the gallery owner will ship any painting anywhere in the country," Bill said.

Sam nodded and feigned interest. "Thank you. I'll keep that in mind."

Zach looked at Connie with a what-am-I-doing-here expression.

It was now or never.

"We still can't get over what happened to Jeff," Connie said, driving the conversation toward the investigation. "Sam has been helping to get the after-school program up and running again this week. Hopefully, Tim and the board of directors will be able to find a worthy replacement."

"Jeff will be hard to replace," Audrey said. "So, Thomas Carmichael..."

Connie interrupted Audrey before she could change the subject. "Jeff had big dreams. When Sam had dinner with him, they talked at length about his plans for the future of the organization."

Connie held Audrey's gaze.

Sam nodded, apparently not quite sure where things were going, but wanting to support Connie.

Audrey squirmed. "I'm sure he did."

"He not only talked about his dreams, but he mentioned the obstacles that stood in his way, as well," Connie added.

Sam looked at Connie and furrowed his brow. "Um, yes. He talked a lot about the challenges he faced."

Connie couldn't blame Sam for not seeing where her questioning was headed, but she was glad he was playing along, anyway.

"His biggest challenge was fundraising," Connie said.

"I would imagine so," Bill said.

"Unfortunately, he had to resort to some unorthodox means to raise funds."

Now Bill was squirming, too. "Well, I wouldn't know anything about that. I left the board of directors a few months ago to focus on my career."

"Our house by the beach doesn't pay for itself," Audrey said. "Bill and I didn't want anything to stand in the way of *our* dreams, either."

"I'm sure all the time Bill spent as a board member ate into valuable time when you could have been working," Sam said.

"You could say that. It's not that we're heartless," Audrey said. "But Bill's life work is his contribution to the art world, not some silly after-school program that only affects a few children's lives."

"Anyone could see that," Connie said. "Bill's career will have a much more lasting impact. I'm sure it's not just about earning a profit. Bill helps artists to make a living, so they, in turn, can bring even more beauty into the world through their art. It's a much bigger contribution to the community, and even the world, than a program that will only benefit a few kids."

Zach and Sam looked at Connie as though she had lost her mind, but Audrey brightened up as though she had finally come across someone who understood her world view.

"Exactly," Audrey said, triumphantly. "Not many people get that, Connie."

"Jeff seemed nice enough," Connie continued, "but he went a little overboard in his role as a mentor. Kate used to tease him about his long hair, saying he spent so much time with the teens that he was starting to look like a teenager."

Audrey chuckled. "Thank goodness he finally cut off that mop."

Suddenly, Audrey realized her mistake. "I mean, that's what I heard."

Connie looked at Zach, who was studying Audrey.

"Audrey, Jeff only cut his hair a few hours before he was murdered," Zach said. "The only people who knew about that were Rachel, Kate, Connie, and Sam."

"Of course," Audrey said. "I think Rachel told me about it. I was really glad to hear he finally cut it off."

Bill was staring dumbfounded at his wife.

Zach snapped into detective mode. "Ma'am, you said that you were happy to have *seen* that Jeff cut his hair. You weren't with your husband at the time of Jeff's murder, were you?"

Bill opened his mouth to speak, but the poor guy was in shock. "No, we weren't together," Bill finally managed to say. "Audrey, how could you? Nobody told us about Jeff's haircut. *I* didn't even know."

"Billy! Stop talking!"

"I asked Audrey to say we were together, because Jeff and I had a falling out and I was afraid that if you learned about it and saw that I didn't have a solid alibi, I'd be a prime suspect. But it never occurred to me that Audrey was the one who killed Jeff and that *I* was giving *her* a false alibi."

"I'll need you both to come to the police station to give a statement," Zach said.

"Don't say another word, Bill," Audrey warned.

But Connie doubted that Bill even heard Audrey. He was staring at his wife with eyes as wide as Frisbees and his jaw hanging open.

Chapter 20

THE FOLLOWING NIGHT, Connie invited her friends over for dinner so they could say goodbye to Sam, since he would be flying home on Saturday afternoon. Connie was thrilled that everyone she had invited, including Kate, Kelly, and Andy, had accepted her invitation. It would be a sizeable crowd for her two-bedroom condo, but as far as Connie was concerned, that was a wonderful problem to have. It meant her circle of amazing friends was growing.

The Millers and Gertrude were the first to arrive, followed by Zach, Stephanie, Gallagher, Kate, and Grace, who came last, because she had been helping Abby at the store until the downtown crowd thinned out.

Kelly and Andy arrived just before Grace, who was looking forward to meeting Andy. Kelly had been ecstatic to learn that Stewart had nothing to do with Jeff's death. Her carefree expression and easy smile revealed her profound relief.

Connie set up a small folding table where the kids could eat, since they wouldn't all fit around the table. The setup reminded Connie of her childhood holidays.

Gertrude insisted on helping Connie, Elyse, and Sam transport the food from the kitchen to the dining room table. When Gertrude picked up the salad bowl, Connie noticed her white medical alert bracelet, but she wasn't sure if she should mention it. She didn't want to draw attention to a sore subject. It turned out she didn't have to.

Gertrude held up her wrist. "My family prevailed on me. I'm not thrilled about it, but wearing this silly thing is easier than dealing with my overprotective family."

"I came clean with Aunt Gertrude and told her about the arrangement I had made with Burt. I didn't want a misunderstanding to damage their friendship," Elyse said.

"Thank goodness I found out before I talked to Burt. I would never have been able to face him again if I had accused him of hitting on me when he was only checking in to be sure I was safe."

"You certainly dodged a bullet there," Sam said.

Connie looped her arm through Sam's, who had just placed a bowl of meatballs and sausages on the table. "I can't believe you're leaving tomorrow. It feels like you just got here."

Sam chuckled. "I don't know about that. In the last two weeks we solved a murder, helped get a non-profit back on its feet, we each got our priorities in order, and you hired a new employee," Sam said, gesturing toward Kelly.

Connie laughed. "I suppose when you put it that way... But I still hate to see you leave."

The night before, while Connie and Sam were decompressing after a long day, Sam decided that he was going to make some major changes once he returned home. He had a long conversation with Janet about hiring someone to manage the day-to-day operations of *Feeding the Hungry*. Working with children again in the after-school program had brought Sam back to his first love and reminded him of why he founded the non-profit to begin with. He preferred to spend his time nurturing *Feeding the Hungry's* partner organizations and developing new relationships.

Janet had also decided to retire early so she could accompany him to on-site visits and offer her skills, as well. Fortunately, Sam's enormous success before he entered the non-profit sector and some wise investments allowed them this flexibility.

"It took a little distance and getting back to my roots to realize why I was burning out," Sam had said to Connie. "I have Jeff's influence to thank for that. Jeff's passion rejuvenated me, and his mistake of trying to do more than he could by blackmailing Bill taught me that, in my own way, I was trying to do more than I originally set out to do. Instead of hiring someone else as the organization grew, I continued to do everything myself."

For her part, Connie also decided to make some changes. She wanted to slow down and enjoy this period in her relationship with Zach. Connie had only been considering hiring part-time help, but since Kelly was available from 9-5 Monday through Friday and needed full-time work so she wouldn't have to work multiple jobs, Connie decided to bite the bullet and hire Kelly full-time. In addition to giving Connie more flexibility, it would also mean more time to expand her Fair Trade session without overextending herself and cutting too much into her personal life.

Once the lasagna, meat, and salad were on the table, they sat down to eat.

"I can't thank you enough for everything you did to help solve my brother's murder," Kate said to Connie, Sam, Zach, and Josh. "A huge burden has been lifted knowing that Audrey is behind bars and, despite everything, I'm happy to know the truth. My brother wasn't a bad person. He simply got caught up in trying to help the underdog. I don't agree with what he did, but it shouldn't have cost him his life."

"At least now he can rest in peace," Kelly added.

"I have some more good news," Kate said. "I'm thrilled to announce that Trevor decided to take over as executive director of the after-school program. Tim called an emergency board meeting this afternoon, after Trevor told him that he wanted to leave his job as a case manager to take over for Jeff. The board voted unanimously to hire him. Tim called me with the good news just before I got here."

"That's fabulous news," Sam said. "Trevor is the best person to honor Jeff's memory and wishes."

"In addition," Kate said, "Bill was so upset about what Audrey did that he made a large contribution to the program's annuity, and he asked to be reinstated on the board of directors. Apparently, everything that happened shocked him into making some serious changes in his own life, as well."

"If it's any consolation," Connie said to Kate, "Jeff's life not only had a big impact on Bill and Trevor, but also on Sam and me. It was the impetus for my hiring Kelly and for Sam making some changes in his own organization."

"And on me, as well." Kelly said. "I decided to give Stewart another chance. In hindsight, I think I was unfair to him. I accused him of something before I had all the facts. When I learned that you all thought Jeff and I were having an affair, I realized how easy it was to get the wrong impression of someone, and I did a little more digging. It appears that I jumped to some false conclusions about Stewart being unfaithful. We have some trust issues to work through, but we are both committed to giving it our all."

"I, for one, am thrilled that this tragedy brought Kelly to us," Grace said, smiling at Kelly and then at Andy, who was sneaking Ginger a piece of a meatball. "We get to have Kelly and Andy in our lives, and Kelly's extensive retail experience will make her a valuable asset to *Just Jewelry*."

"When I told Abby that I hired Kelly, she burst out laughing," Connie said. "She said if it weren't for my meddling in murder investigations, I'd have no employees in my store. She pointed out that all my employees were formerly murder suspects."

Grace had been under suspicion with the police when a man was thrown to his death from her balcony two years ago, and Abby was a member of Connie's first jewelry-making class, which ended in the murder of one of her students.

Zach put his arm around Grace's shoulders. "Yeah, sorry about the whole accusing-you-of-murder thing. But in our defense, Josh and I didn't know you two years ago like we do now, and Hank *was* thrown from *your* balcony."

"It sounds like it's going to be exciting working for Connie," Kelly said.

Elyse smiled. "You can count on that. There hasn't been a dull moment since Connie moved to Sapphire Beach.

"I can't take the suspense anymore," Sam said to Zach and Josh. "Tell us what happened with Audrey. We heard on the news this morning that she was arrested."

"Audrey's comment about Jeff's haircut pointed us in the right direction," Zach said. "We hadn't searched Bill's and Audrey's garage, because we didn't have evidence for a warrant, and they alibied one another. But when we searched the premises early this morning, we found DNA evidence both in their garage and in the driveway. There was also DNA evidence that linked Audrey to Jeff's car."

"It turns out," Josh continued, "that Jeff went to their house to talk to Bill, but he was out at the bar, so he found Audrey alone. She tried to convince him to drop his blackmailing scheme, but when he refused, she knocked him out by hitting him with a vase and dragged him to his car, which she left running in the garage. Once he had died, she put her bike in his trunk, drove the car with Jeff's body inside to an out-of-the-way road, and bicycled home."

"What about Bill?" Sam asked. "Is he going to jail for selling stolen art?"

Josh shook his head. "He told us everything he knew, which wasn't much, since he didn't know the identity of the art thief who sold him the paintings. Since he cooperated with Jeff's murder investigation, we agreed not to press charges. But Bill did mention that he's going to put his house up for sale in light of what happened. Trevor found out what was going on through a mutual friend at the art exhibition, and he waited for Bill in the police station lobby for hours while Bill gave us his statement. They seem to have rekindled their friendship. It's hard to know for sure so early on, but it looks like Bill is going to change his life for the better."

While Josh and the others were caught up in conversation, Zach leaned in and whispered in Connie's ear. "I'm glad you hired Kelly. Hopefully, now that Sam is heading back to Massachusetts and this case has been closed, we can spend some more time together. There's something I've been wanting to ask you, but I've been waiting for the right time."

Connie rested her head on his shoulder. "What is it?"

"Not yet," Zach replied. "We'll talk when the time is right. Right now, let's enjoy the company of our friends."

The End

Next Book in this Series

Book 10: *Passion and Poison*

Paperback bundles are available at Angela's store. Visit: store.angelakryan.com/collections/paperback-bundles to save with a bundle.

Individual books are available on Amazon.

OR

Free Prequel: *Vacations and Victims.*

Meet Concetta and Bethany in the
Sapphire Beach prequel.

Available in ebook or PDF format only at:
BookHip.com/MWHDFP

Stay in touch!

Join my Readers' Group for periodic updates,
exclusive content, and to be notified of new
releases. Enter your email address at:
BookHip.com/MWHDFP

OR

Email:
angela@angelakryan.com

Facebook:
facebook.com/AngelaKRyanAuthor

Post Office:
Angela K. Ryan, John Paul Publishing, P.O. Box 283,
Tewksbury, MA 01876

MEET THE AUTHOR

Angela K. Ryan is the author of the *Sapphire Beach Cozy Mystery Series* and the *Seaside Ice Cream Shop Mysteries*. She writes clean, feel-good cozies for readers who love humor, lots of twists and turns, and happy-dance endings.

When she is not writing, Angela enjoys the outdoors, especially kayaking, stand-up paddleboarding, snowshoeing, and skiing. She lives in Massachusetts and loves all four of the New England seasons, but she looks forward to regular escapes to the white, sandy beaches of southwest Florida, where her mother resides.

It is fitting that Angela's two series take place in fictitious seaside towns in Massachusetts and Florida. These small towns would be idyllic if it weren't for all the bodies that keep turning up!

Angela dreams of one day owning a Cavalier King Charles Spaniel like the sweet pup in her *Sapphire Beach Series*, but she isn't home enough to take care of one. So, for now, lives vicariously through one of her main characters, Connie.

Made in the USA
Columbia, SC
20 May 2024